THE INNER D

BY ANN HUNT

A PSYCHOLOGICAL DRAMA

CHAPTER 1

Summer sat with her head turned as she watched the city she'd grown up in disappear into the distance behind her. Now she could relax in her roomette on the Amtrak train to Chicago.Then onto New Orleans where she hoped to disappear in Party City. She'd made her mind up never to go back to Seattle. Looking at her watch it was just gone one am, her stepfather should be hopping made looking for her by now.

She couldn't believe it had all happened in such a short time, only three and a half hours ago. She was glad she'd packed half her things weeks before and hide them in her closet as she'd decided to leave home as soon as she was 16.

She'd read a book months earlier about a girl getting a new Identity card and birth certificate so she could run away. And it worked as she'd bee'n able to get herself a new birth certificate months back."Planning was everything". Even down to going to a grave yard, and looking for a grave stone with the same birth date as her's but a year old than herself and of course the same sex. She'd been able to find a mother and daughter. And checked their records at the town hall. As she hoped the new certificate would make her a year older than her true age of 15.

She then asked at the council offices for a new birth certificate, saying she'd lost her old one. She'd had to give her real address. But as usual no one was home only herself when it came. Then she got a new Identity card so she could work. She'd intended to go just after her sixteenth birthday in a few months. But things came to a head with her stepfather once again.

That night was imprinted in her mind. What happened at 7pm that Thursday, her mother left to go to a yoga club with the girls. So her stepfather decided as her mother was out that he'd have some sexual fun once again by assault her. Something he'd done since he'd married her mother when she was 11. Only she'd told herself after the last time no more. So this time she was ready for him when he came in her room in his robe. "she knew he was naked under it". And she knew straight away why he was in her room without even turning around to look at him.

Her heart started racing as she anticipated his next move, as he walked over to her while she was sitting with her back to him at her deck, she'd been doing her homework. She suddenly felt his hot breath on her neck, this time she wouldn't let him assault her. She was determined to stop him as her heart raced fast. As he leaned over her and went to put his hand down her top. Mercedes grabbed her nail scissors and plunged them into his right ear as he fondled her breast.

He screamed out, but instead of moving away from her then, he yelled out how dare you, So you want to play dirty do you pulling the scissors out and dropping them on the floor.

Blood was pouring from his ear, only it didn't seem to stop him as he said two can play at that game grabbed her by the throat.
As she choked and started to pass out he suddenly became faint and release her throat as he dropped to the floor.

He lay there unconscious so she thought? She picked up the scissors and wiped them on his robe and put them in her rucksack that lay on the floor. Now she was in a panic as this was not how she meant things to go grabbing the rest of her clothes and Tablet, also her phone taking out the sim card so he could not track her. And stood looking at him. Just because you're Mayor of Seattle and well loved, so it seemed by all. You think you could do know wrong but not this time. You told me once that money can buy a lot of silence and people. And mother, when I told her years back that you were rapping me. She never believed me.

So that was that for me "Mercedes" my real name" you said was fitting as you could ride me like that car. I had to live with being raped when every you felt like it. Now who has the upper hand?

While riding me you'd say I was you're little Mercedes, like you're Mercedes saloon car. No more as now I'm free of you and that car's name. From now on I'll be known as Summer like the little girl who had died with her mother in a car crash. I hope to do my new name proud, Summer Dalla-Rosa a lovely name from Brazil.

Stepping over his body on the floor she opened her jewel box and took out the silver cross and chain with an Amethyst stone in the middle and tiny flowers carved into the silver. It was something she treasured, as it was the last thing her grandmother had given her before she died. Her stepfather disapproved of her wearing it as he wasn't catholic like grandmother and mother. She then put the cross around her neck never to take it off, as it had belonged to her great-grandmother before her gran as well, and now it was her's.

Summer's mind was now cleared of it all for good. And went back to watching the lights in the country side through the moving train window. It would take two days to complete her journey to New Orleans with one change in Chicago.

God she suddenly hoped she'd saved enough money as she had to leave sooner than she had planned. There had been a couple hundred dollars in her stepfathers wallet that she'd found on his bedside table. And mother's diamond neckless in her mothers jewel box that she treasured. Hopping it would keep her in food for a

4

while. She knew what to do with the neckless, separate the diamonds and melt down the gold. She'd seen enough movies on TV to know that. The diamonds she'd sell one or two at a time so as not to make the Jewellery suspicious. And she'd go to different ones if possible.

She hoped to find a cheap Bed and Breakfast to stay at, until she could find a cheap flat or house to rent in the poorer district. As she knew New Orleans had a lot of them going by NCIS New Orleans she'd watched weekly on television. The flat would have to wait a bit till she had found a job singing in a bar or club.

Being the lead singer in the school choir and also sang solo she hoped would help her get a job. Singing was her passion she loved it, It had got her through the bad times at home, it was her escape from her nightmare life. Also hoped as she was told several times by boys that she was pretty with her tall slim boyish figure and waist length black hair and large dark brown eye's, that the club Owners would give her a chance just by her looks. Then when they heard her sing they would hire her for her voice not just her looks? She had little experience of the outside world but it couldn't be worst than her home life.

She'd taken some of her mothers make up so she'd look older than 16 on her new identity card. Mascara blusher and lip stick as well as moisturiser, her mother had lot's so surely she'd not even notice. So decided to get up and go and put some on before she got to her stop.

Took the small bag from her hand luggage and went into her cabins small cubicle with its tiny hand basin and mirror and put it all on. Remembering her mother had forbid her to use it till she was 18, as she looked at her self in the mirror. She didn't like the feel of the moisturiser on her skin and hoped she'd get use to it, as the make up did make her look older.

Summer's mind went back to her mother and wondered how she might be feeling right now. Surely she'd know the reason I'd run away. After all those years she had looked the other way while he rape her. More than likely her mother would be more upset loosing her precious neckless that loosing her daughter she thought.

Summer sat back down in the carriage and suddenly started to cry. Something she hadn't done in years as she sobbed into her hands, and cried till she had know more tears left.

Got up and walked back into the shower to splash water on her face. As she looked up into the mirror, all the makeup had run down her face. And she suddenly found herself laughing as she started to wiped the makeup off. From now on she would only use the blusher and eyeshadow she told her self as she walked back into the carriage.

It was now gone 2am she should try and get some sleep as Chicago was many hours away, as she lay her tied body on top of the covers on the top bunk. The 3143 miles would soon pass and her journey would be over as she fell sound asleep to the rhyme of the train.

She awoke to the sound of people in the corridor and looked out the widow. The train was now at Chicago station. She'd sleep a lot longer than normal. So quickly jumped down and gathered her things and followed the people out on to the platform, then through the barrier to find the New Orleans line for the other half of her journey to her new life. She had no time to change or even wash. And she so wanted to pee, and her stomach also made a rumbly noise, as it was well pass lunch time. She told herself that everything would have to wait till she was on the New Orleans train.

Hoping it had a restaurant or something as it was a much longer journey than to Chicago was.

CHAPTER 2

Summer stood on the platform in New Orleans Union station and suddenly realised that she really was free at last as she took her first steps to her new life, as she walked towards the entrance.

When she'd left Seattle it had been dark and chilly, now it was bright sunshine and very warm for April.

The billboard outside said Loyola Avenue, looking around the area to find a bus stop. The area she noticed was very open and green. She saw that the bus stop was over the other side of the green area next to a lane. So gathered her luggage and walked over to it. And as she put her luggage down on the pavement she noticed another wide green area where 2 tall statue's of different cube shapes and sizes also colours all balanced on each other, very different from anything she'd seen, and they looked like they were made of plastic. They were nothing like any statue's she'd seen before. She felt it was more for children but she liked them. It gave her a warm feeling.

Opposite the bus stop the City begun with modern buildings of different heights, not the New Orleans she'd seen on Television. And hoped the rest would be more like she seen in NCIS New Orleans. Even the Palm trees were different in that area with thick trunks and heavy green foliage. Unlike Los Angeles that they had visited for a vacation a couple of years back. This was not what she had expected.

A bus pulled up beside her. And she got on board. She'd notice outside it read it was going to St Charles Avenue then down 2 other streets she had not caught the name's of. She would stay on till the end, then ask the bus driver if he knew where she could find out about B & B's. After all she was not in a hurry any more.

She suddenly changed her mind and after looking out the window pass several beautiful houses, decided to get off half way down Esplanade Avenue instead of the bottom of it where the bus turned around to go back.

Before getting off she asked the driver about B and B's. He told her that at the bottom of the Avenue was the river, so if you go down to the corner then turn right along that road, about 10 minutes along is the French Market, and if you walk for another 10 minutes you come to Jackson Square where it all happens. Places to stay this time of year are high priced Hotels.

If you stay in this area off Esplanade there are two streets on the left side were you might get cheap B and B's or Guest house.
Then there is the quieter part of Royal Street, also the quiet part of Bourbon Street all on the left. Not the on the right of the avenue as that's in the French quarter area like all the roads on the right.
Remember the roads off the left side of Esplanade might have cheap places to stay. And also in that area is the famous frenchman Street which is mostly music clubs and bars, but does have a few places to stay.

Summer decided to take his advice and walked along till she came to Royal Street on the left. And walked along it a short distance when she saw In the distance a large colourful flower covered building which looked like something out of the wild west, all made of wood with its veranda and steps leading up to it's main doors. It was all covered from top to toe in climbing flowering plants in pots up against the veranda on the side street part. It also had shrubs in pots all with red flowers growing both on the street side and above on a long Balcony. It looked like something out of a fairy-tail story.

As she stared at it she could see tiny fairy lights all over the building and roof as well. She loved what she was seeing and couldn't stop stared, as she'd never scene such a place.

Suddenly a woman appeared in her forty's dressed in a long colourful hippy skirt and red top and sandals. Her long vivid red hair was braided n a plait.

She'd seen the young girl staring and decided to check her out. Can I help you miss in a rich southern accent? If you're looking for a place to bed for the night we charge 99 dollars including breakfast. You won't find cheaper in April what with the 2 music festivals.

Summer stared at this woman, As she'd never seen anyone quit like her, and it seemed she liked red. What the hell she thought the woman looks friendly enough so asked her if she could have a room for two weeks.

The woman smiled and replied yes of course follow me.

Summer walked up the steps and into what looked like a music club with it's bar and stage in the corner, not like a guest house at all. Nerve's she told the lady she only had cash on her not bank cards?

No need to be nerve's here, and yes cash is fine as she walked behind the bar and took a key from a board on the wall. I'll show you to your room, your'e lucky that we have one left after the couple who were coming canceled at the last minute from Europe. So now with you we have a full house as usual for April May.

Summer counted out one thousand four hundred dollars, which left her with only a couple of hundred left as she'd under estimate the cost of places to stay there, as she'd never done any of this on her own before.

Whats your name child, mine is Madam Apollo goddess of music, and I run this place as she handed her the key to her room. Need your name for my registry child?

Summer Dalla-Rosa taking out her ID card and handed it to her knowing full well there was nothing wrong with it, except it was not her real name. It had worked at Seattle Station when she bought her ticket so it should be fine now she thought?

Madam Apollo looked at it then counted out four hundred dollars and handed the card and money back to her saying we have a discount for over a week's stay. Now let me show you to your room, then if you would, please join me for lunch in the bar, breakfast is in the restaurant next door that I own and they do great cheap food.

Summer plucked up the courage to ask her something as she was shown her room, which was colourful just like Madam, and spacious with a queen size bed covered in colourful bedding mostly red, very large television and an equally small fridge and coffee maker, also a hair dryer which she was pleased about as she had forgotten to packed hers. It's more than I had hope for Madam Apollo. Do you mind me asking you do you have live bands here. As I am looking for a job singing full time?

We'll girl if you sing as good as you look maybe one of the bands here will give you go, starting with the one this evening here. I'll leave you now to unpack.

Summer put her luggage on the bed an wen't out onto the balcony, and stood looking at the area around the guest house which was in Faubourg Marigny a working class area but with the best streets for music club's, Frenchman Street being the best one, and it was only a block away.

The other half of Royal Street across Esplanade Avenue was in the french quarter more a tourist area with shops selling tourist wears so she'd read in her Lonely planet tourist guide. She'd come to the right area if she hope to sing with a band. Went back inside and unpacked her stuff. So far things had gone better than she'd hoped crossing her fingers.

Summer took her leather case that had some songs inside that she'd composed herself, may be Madam will let me play one after Lunch, looked around her room and went out on to the landing and locked her door and walked down into the bar. And saw Madam intensely talking to two young black youths. On seeing Summer she introduced them to her. It turned out they looked after the cleaning and maintenance of the place.

Cheap labour crossed Summer mind as they wern't much older than herself. Then another young girl appeared this time from a side door leading from the restaurant, carrying their lunch for the two of them on a large wooden tray. And put it down at Madam's private table in a corner next to the bar.

Come child lunch has arrived, dismissing the 3 youths without a thankyou. As they both sat Madam then poured her a glass of sweet red wine. Quick as a flash Summer's told her she was a buddhist so did not drink alcohol.

"She wasn't" but Madam did not know that. And in a City that makes it money on booze being a Buddhist seemed the best Idea. And New Orleans did have a Buddhist Temple outside the City, as they had a big Vietnamese community living there in New Orleans east and Algiers areas she'd read about them in Lonely planet. So being buddhist seemed a good idea as she was only 15 pretending to be 16 so no drink.

Madam didn't seem to mind and said that was fine with her not drinking.Then asked her a direct question why she'd left home as she couldn't be any more than 16,18, was she right? Summer said she was 16, and left home because her stepfather had raped her since she could remember. But decided to say know more on the subject.

Madam was taken aback by the girls frankness, and told her she'd keep it to her self. You have come to the right place, as I also was raped by my father. So I ran away much younger than you at 14 just after he started to assault me. I was taken in by the christian charity of St Francis, they took care of me and sent me to school and gave me a safe place to live. I never told any one outside the church charity. At what age were you when it started?

Summer had told know one up till now, and wondered what she'd say if she told her she was 11 when it started. Looked Madam straight in the eyes and said 11 and waited for her reaction.

Madam was silent for a good few minutes before she spoke. You should have gone to the police long ago or the church like me. God you were young.

My stepfather has an important public job, so know one would have believe me, my mother didn't. So the last time he did it I left to come here. I'm never going back there.

Your secret is safe with me child. To night I'll get you a slot to sing before Davis band go's on. Davis is a lady's man and likes to put his hands on your butt while he is talking to you if he fancy's you. And the way you look he will, so be careful. Why don't you go and sing something, so I know I am not wasting my time talking music? Do you play piano as well?

Summer finished her last bite of food and washed it down with the bottle of water, got up said nothing in reply and walked over to the small stage with its permanent old tatty piano, and jumped up on to the stage. Opened up the piano and ran her fingers over it. The sound was a bit raw but not as bad she thought as it looked on the outside. Poor piano she told it lovingly running her hands over the wood before settling on the tatty stool. Opened her leather folder and put a sheet of music on the piano.

Nervously she looked around the bar it had about a dozen punters in there, as she started to make the tatty old piano come to life and sing as she sang. Giving it everything she'd got.A hush suddenly came over the bar as the punters stood or sat silently listening to the voice of pure velvet coming from a beautiful young tall girl with long black hair and a boyish figure sing like an angel.

Madam couldn't believe her ears as she'd not heard a voice like that in years. It had a sad hint to it she felt. As she looked at her she could see lots of dollar signs "yes lots" She was going to make her rich while she managed her voice in the different clubs and bars. And tonight would be the start of better things to come for both of them as she smiled at her, and said   Softy to herself she said you're going to be my ticket out of New Orleans, Las Vegas here we come.

Summer had enough of the bar with it's heavy drink and sweaty smell about it, as it had no air conditioning something she was not use to. And as it was only just gone five she decided to go to Frenchman Street and check out the bars there, maybe find out if any are hiring a solo artist on piano in stead of joining a band. She didn't want to tie herself down to one club or one band unless she had to. Madam seemed to think solo for now was best.

Turned out Frenchman Street was one very long Street with a wide cut-de-sac ally half way down. Where there was held an art market and CD's, also hand made Jewellery every afternoon and evening.

Summer walked along the Street, passing Creole food restaurants and a voodoo shop. Then she came to a small club with a sign hanging outside with a black cat on it, it read the Spotted Cat open 4pm till 2am Monday till Friday then 3pm Saturday and Sunday. Opposite on the other side of the narrow street was the Sting Harbour, both Jazz clubs only one looked as if it where a sweatbox kind of place with it's plastic every where even spirit cups. The other a swish martini spot. Both were open now, but she'd give them a miss for now.

Summer came to another side street St Claude, down it she could see a sign hanging out side a club saying the HI HO Lounge 6 till 3 opening time, she'd try there tomorrow evening as well as she crossed over St Claude and continued down Frenchman till she came to D.B.A Club, a swanky club so the gentleman outside it was saying to a group of punters hanging around, it's the best place in town with top music acts playing everything from jazz rock and blues. You name it they have top bands that are playing in the coming weeks. Summer thought that sounded great for her being solo and they were open at 5pm looking at her watch it was nearly six now.

They also stayed open an extra hour she noticed as well. She'd hang about for a while to see if she could get them to hear her some time, before going back to the Guest house and change for her solo tonight before the Davis band went on.

She'd only been in New Orleans a couple of hours and things were looking up. Fingers crossed the proprietor at D.B.A would let her play something for him on the piano in a minute as she stood inside by the stage near where the decent shiny piano stood and waited to be noticed.

Standing there she thought back to Seattle and her parents, and wondered if they cared that she'd left home? Wondered if her stepfather had called the police about her missing and that she attacked him with her scissors. Her stepfather would have to give a reason for her assaulting him, and she was sure he'd never do that.

Just then a voice behind her asked if she was waiting for someone as she had no drink. Summer turned to see a smart funky looking thick set coloured man with hair tied back, and a goaty beard staring down at her, he must be at least 6 foot 3 or4 she thought as she looked up to him as she was 5 foot 11.

Summer replied sorry but she wondered if she could sing and play on that beautiful piano as she was after a solo spot in his club. The tall man was greeted by another black man less impressive. And by their conversation she heard, the funky guy was the owner. So she took the bull by the horns to ask him once again, after the other man went over to the bar. Asked if he had a spot for a solo singer, giving him her name.

Summer nervously stood looking up at him and waited for him to speak.

The guy stepped back a little and looked her up and down then said if you need a job miss we need a waitress?

Summer cleared her throat and said she was looking for a solo spot singing one or two nights. I can play a mean piano and have been told I have a good singing voice and waited again for him to reply.

The other guy on hearing the conversation had come over by now and said she's a stunner that would bring in the punters even if she can't sing, but I'll leave her with you and walked to the back of the club and disappeared throw a door. The Funky guy just stood and stared at her, then spoke, well you have kerb appeal I'll give you that. Come back tomorrow at 10am and I'll hear you sing and play a mean piano okay?

Summer couldn't believe her luck and said she'd be there thanking him. Then she blurted out that she would be playing tonight at the Balcony guest house at 8pm. Then turned and walked out. Turned and said oh by the way my name is Summer Dalla-Rosa.

Out side she quickened her pace back to the Guest house pleased with her self. Then changed her mind as she looked at her watch she still had a couple of hours before she needed to get back, so decided to walk to the French market and by the Mississippi River to see if they sold ice cream.

The French Market was nothing like she thought it would be. There was no fruit and veg, it was all tourist trinkets and leather bags and wallets all for the tourist. There was a stall selling cakes and pastries. Summer bought two delicious looking Pastries. Next door looked like a juice bar till she read the board above the back of the counter.

It had juice in it also mixed spirit's of some kind. They all had two or three different spirits in them topped with a cherry or olive. They looked good and seemed to be selling well. She pinched herself hard, so she'd remember she was only 15 not 21 as she took a big bite of her pastie and walked out of the Market. Up some steps behind a group of shops and down some more on to a promenade beside the river. The air smelt fresh and cool altho it was well over 20 degrees. After the smells of the City with it's spices and the smell of drink on the street's. She was looking for somewhere to get a cold drink even a coffee would be nice but no not along those shops.

There was seating along the promenade so she sat and eat her pastries and sipped the bottled water she'd bought from a vender selling from a large covered freezer box at the back of his bike. She'd love a milkshake and wondered if anywhere sold it. A couple of elderly woman walked towards her bench. So she decided to ask them if they knew any where she could get one.

The ladies were only too pleased to help, and told her that if she kept walked along the sea wall till she came to a carpark that had black and white tiles on the ground. "Very expensive tiles bought with Katrina money by the council said one of them disapproving". You will find two sets of stairs going up either side there, take either and you'r see in front of you at the top Jackson Square. Go down the left set of stairs turn and keep walking right for 5 minutes and your find just what you are looking for.

Summer thanked them and continued walking till she came to the very loud tiles layed down in the car park, she'd never seen glazed tiles in a car park like them, they looked out of place. And understood why the two ladies spoke about them the way they did, as they looked a waste of money.

At the top of the stairs the area was a balcony so you could see opposite it the famous Cathedral in Jackson Square and a small park area in front of it, and around the park were railings. And from what she could make out on the railing hanging there were paintings. And people seemed to be buying them. She could also hear music coming from across there outside the White Cathedral as well. She decided to walked down the left steps from the balcony turned and walked towards the ice cream parlour that the ladies had told her about. And there it was just as the ladies had said as she walked up the steps and throw the doors up to the counter. It was like stepping back in time as she stopped in front of a counter where there was every kind of ice cream you could think of and some she hadn't. She took her time and ordered herself a banana and Chocolate milkshake also a strawberry and fudge ice cream sundae and sat at a small tiled round table with it's red leather stool and waited while they were being prepared in front of her. The whole experience cost her fourteen dollar's which seemed a lot to her but well worth it as she tucked into them both smiling and eat them simultaneously before going back to the Guest house. She felt very full and also a little sick after all she'd eaton that afternoon. She wasn't use to eating so much at the same time.

Outside the parlour she realised that the Guest house was a fair distance walk away. She'd walked without thinking of how far she was walking. And the way she felt and also by the time she'd walked back there, she'd be late and not have time to change and prepare for her session singing at the piano. She'd not meant to take so long, as she started walking back towards Jackson Square before the long walk to Esplanade Avenue and up it to Royal Street.

Parked in front of St Anns Street next to Jackson Square were bike's for two with drivers for hire, a dollar a mile saved her walking she thought. Also how much can it cost to Royal Street. It can only be a couple of miles away. So she hired one and sat on the seat at the back, gave the address as she wanted to get going. Sat back and relaxed as the rider set off in that direction as she started to pedal, as she still felt a little sick.

Outside the Balcony Guest house and bar there was a crowd gathered watching, as a group of musicians were taken there instruments inside to set up, Davis band had arrived as she pulled up near them.

The bike driver asked for twelve dollars fare. And as she was late she paid it, much against her judgement as she believed five or six dollars seemed fair as it was only a couple of miles away not twelve if it was one dollar a mile.

Madam spotted Summer outside, and sent one of her bar staff to hurry her up as she was very late and the band was due on in 10 minutes. And if She really wanted to sing in clubs she'd have to be on time in future.

Summer hurried inside and up to her room to change, there was no time to shower. This was not how she hoped her first session on stage would go, but nothing she could do about it now as she change into a long colourful skirt and white brocade lace blouse but kept her sandals on. Got an antacid and put it in a glass of water to fizz then drank it down as she knew she shouldn't have eaton two pastries and the stuff at the milk shake pantry, plus the lunch before. God she hoped she wouldn't be sick, or effect her voice as she cleaned her teeth, sprayed her mothers Miss Dior perfume over herself. She was ready and it had only taken 10 minutes as she undid her hair brushed it and left it loose down her back. This was it, she had to make a good impression on the punters so word would get round and she'd get more work in the area's clubs.

Davis and the other band members were ready to start, as she came into the bar and over to the stage. Followed on her heels by Madam. Where were you you'er late girl not a good start to a singing career? Get on the stage and give them hell girl, go for it. David won't mind you singing with them as it's too late for you to go solo unless you want to wait till tomorrow?

Summer climb up on stage she still felt quinsy as she turned to the dilapidated piano and said god I hope for an old boy I can make you sing as she waited for the band to start to play a Jazz piece she knew and she started to sing, then without stopping straight into another piece.

Till the interval for the band where she played her own piece she'd written herself Blue Waters. A very modern jazz piece. She had run over time as she stopped and looked around at the punters who had been silent all that time she had played. Her voice had not been at it's best and was dry as she needed a drink of water. Looked over towards the bar and made a drink jester to a barman. Davis instead got up and came over and gave her a clear glass that looked like water. She took a gulp and swallowed not realising it was spiced Rum till it hit her throat and went down making her choke. And it was not what her stomach needed right now as the antacid hadn't worked as she climbed back down and waited to hear what Davis thought of her voice, oh how she'd wished she'd not had that milkshake and ice cream soda.

Davis had already started talking to Madam about her while she was she choking. Then said girl "liked" your voice and you play a mean piano. Now it is our turn and the reason people are here. Why don't you take a rest for a while and then join in with us again, I'm sure you'r be able to follow us joining in singing in chorus?

Summer handed him back the still half full glass of rum and said she'd love too. And watched him down it in one and up end the glass on top of a table near by. She looked at her watch it was now nearly 11 pm she'd been playing for nearly 1 hour three quarters and so took a break of 15 minutes as Davis and his band got settled back into there places standing on stage for their last session of the evening.

Summer sat at the piano and listened to their first couple of songs, then the next one she listen to the lines of music before realising that she knew that song and joined in on the piano.

At the bar Madam was a little disappointed at Summers voice the first part of the evening, but it got better going alone, so she thought it was most likely nerves on her part, and was pleased with her find. Summer would go far with her talent and make Madam lots of money. Davis also loved the girls talent and why not as she looked good as well.

I'll have to get her a new wardrobe of clothes thought madam. And was sure she'd be able to find some items revealing Summers assets at Vintage Wears in the French Quarter. It would be worth spending a little on the girl as she watched the punters put money in the over sized brandy glass on the bar when they bought drinks. And there was the cover charge to get in the Club, she could put it up when news gets around there's a new voice in town.

The band's money for playing didn't include Summer payment. And the more punters she brings in the bar meant more punters buying drinks, so it was good all round. Madam felt real pleased with her self.

Tomorrow she'd contact other clubs in the area as she was sure news of Summer had started to traveled in New Orleans music scene, she'd ask them if they would book her for a one night stand. That's when she'd take her managers fee out.

Summer could have a share of the nights fee from the money in the glass at the bar. That was when she'd make more money with the drinks sales. All this went though Madams mind was unknown to Summer who was happily playing sweet music on the piano but not singing now as she still felt a little sickly.

The next morning she got up early as she'd only slept a little, even after going to bed at 3am. Things had gone so well so far that her mind could not believe it had happened and it played on her mind. Showered and dressed in slacks and top she grabbed a coffee and bun from Madams pantry glanced at her watch it was nine am. She'd go for a walk around New Orleans to get her baring before the crowds arrive. If I'm going to make it my home then I have to check the place out.

Last night Madam had told her to stay around the bar in the morning as she wanted to talk to her about gigs. But from now on she was not going to let any one tell her what to do, and in any case she had an appointment at D.B.A club at 10 and know way was she going to tell Madam about it. Or let madam tell her what to do about gigs as she was doing okay so far on her own. And after all she was a paying quest in Madams guest house, something Madam seemed to have forgotten. Also Madam did seem a little annoyed as she asked her why she'd not sang along with the band for the last half hour but just played piano.

Now she was off to look around before Madam got up patting an old thin looking cat inside the main door, do you live her old girl I'll bring you back a tin of tuna rubbing the cats head as the cat rubbed it self around her legs. Must go now puss.

She'd seen yesterday that there were horse drawn carriages you could ride on a tour around New Orleans and she fancied that, as she looked at her watch it was just gone 9 she'd enjoy walking around the French Quarter till the interview at the new club. She'd go on a ride after her interview this morning. Mustn't forget the cat food as she saw another tabby cat cross her path.

That part of New Orleans looked even better than on the TV series and was glad she'd decided to come here. Then she started wondering again how her mother was right now and her stepfather the bastard, served him right as she watch people setting up there paintings on the railings in Jackson Square. I must put them out of my head if I want to move on.

She walked along the other half of Royal Street with it's creole town houses with their wonderful iron balconies, and passed shops each selling different things for the tourist. Came to some more small section of railings by an alley way with artist painting's hanging from them. On the other side of the narrow lane was a grocers, so decided to go in and buy some things to go in her room as eating out was not an option for her both money wise and her tummy.

The grocers on the corner of Royal Street in the French quarter had everything you could think off crammed in to it's tiny space. For 30 dollars she'd bought quite a lot of food, now she'd have to carry it with her to Frenchman Street for her interview before going back to her room with her things. Something she hadn't thought about before buying the stuff. Mustn't impulse buy she told herself.

Summer hoped that when she did arrive back, Madam wouldn't see her as she hoped to be in and out as she wanted to go for that ride. Walking back the way she'd come through Jackson Square she saw the bikes for hire, a dollar a mile and thought to herself that's a lie as she passed them.

As she turned into Frenchman Street her arms were now aching. A head was the D.B.A. club and her interview. She suddenly felt nerve's about playing, she wasn't at the Balcony. For some reason this felt more important as she stopped at the door and waited for one of the men inside to open it as they cleared away last evenings glass's.

The tall good looking black owner of the club saw her and came over to open it. He smiled on seeing the shopping bags she was carrying with her. Anything that needs to go in the fridge while you have your interview miss?

Summers had yogurts and some chocolate drinks that more than likely were turning warm. So replied yes sir I have a couple.

Give them here, I'll get one of my people to put them in the cold room with the alcohol. By the way what's your name again miss?

Summer Dalla-Rosa sir.

Mine is Moses Brooks, call me Moses every one does here and I'll call you Summer. Now we have that out of the way, where have you sung before? And how old are you as you look very young?

Sixteen sir and I'v only played at Balcony Guest house Club bar here. And at school as a solo artist with the choir. We won several prices as she nervously looked up at him gosh he was beautiful.

Now Summer let me see what you have got, we don't have any one to play on the piano to accompany you sorry.

I don't need it Moses as I accompany my self walking to the large stage where a piano stood and several other musical items, climb up and walked over to it, lifted up the lid. It was a nicer looking piano than Madams she thought running her fingers along the key board, it also sounded better as she sat down on the stool and started to play her own piece of music that she'd written her self and started to sing. Her voice was fine today as was her tummy as she got lost in the music and went from one song to another till Moses put his hand on her shoulder making her jump, turning on him she pushing him hard away from her with her fisted before she realised who it was. Quickly said sorry as she explained she got lost in the music.

"Which was part true the other part was that she thought he was her stepfather for a minute" only she couldn't tell Moses that.

Moses knew the sign of sexual harassment, and knew why she had been like that, as he'd dealt with girls who have had dealings with predators. Maybe when she trusts him she will tell him her story?

We'll Summer you have a good voice and even better musical fingers, so I'd like you to play Friday and Saturday night around 10 for an hour. I'll pay you each time you play. How does that sound?

How much will be determent by how well you go down with the customers. Now be off with you as I have business in the City. I'll drop you off at the guest house if you like on my way. See you at 9 30 Friday, give you a chance to see what the atmosphere is like in here.

Summer thanked him collected all her things and walked with him to his car. Inside she was feeling in high spirits. Really elated and wondered what Madam would say when she told her. At 6 pm she'd try the HI HO lounge and see if they would give her a spot.

She got out at the cross road near the Guest house and walked along to it, and managed to get to her room without being seen by Madam, and busying herself putting the things away. The tiny fridge in her room meant the yogurts and milk chocolate drink and butter would stay cold that she'd bought. Now she had to buy a knife for the loaf she'd bought and honey and jam. Also buy a spoon and fork from some where. Not in the French Quarter so maybe the Marigny District here might have normal shops. She'd take a walk across St Claude and up Esplanade Avenue in to Rampart Street. Check the areas map on her phone. Buying food was new to her as was buying anything really. It had all been taken care of by her mother or stepfather. All she ever had to do was just be their dutiful daughter always on show. She hated it unlike her mother who loved being a Mayor's partner. She quit enjoyed doing things on her own, expressly when it went well.

She wondered how long it would take before she stopped thinking about them, as all she wanted to do was get on with her new life. Slowly she walked out into the hall and down into the bar area, looking as she went to see if Madam was around. Again there was no sign of her so Summers rushed out into the street and away down Royal Street, then up the very long Esplanade Avenue, then remembered that a Streetcar ran up and down the Avenue and beyond. So she'd use that to get around from now on.

After what seemed hours she'd had got what she needed and some, and liked the Marigny area, which had two other District's wedge in with it, Faubourg and Bywater all three were just what she had hoped.

They had a feeling of the real New Orleans. And the people were a mix or black and Caucasians working class. Now she was of for a carriage ride before going to Hi Ho Lounge.

Summer enjoyed her ride. For the money 60 dollars shared with 4 others made it 15.

She'd grabbed a Po'boy roll full of different meats pickles and salad at a cost of 8 dollars, as it was so very long she'd only been able to eat half and put the other half in her rucksack for later in stead of paying for dinner. She had to be careful of what she spent until she had a regular income. Also she would have to find out about paying tax's. Being a grown up mean't she had to also find out about medical insurance as well. Funny she thought, herself and her friends couldn't wait to be grown up but she realised that there is a lot more to it they'd never thought about, now she had too.

Now she was waiting outside the Club Lounge where men were busying them selves getting ready to open in ten minutes. Summer wondered what the manager looked like as they was a mix of black and Caucasian men in side like the other place.

The ten minutes went quickly and then the doors open. There was no one waiting to go in besides herself as she walked in to a very red closed in room. Even the glass's and candle lights on the table were red. They must be friends with Madam as she loved red she thought. There was a small deep stage with red lighting along the inside. The yellow colour on the outside of the Club was painted along the bottom of the wall. Then further up the walls in several colours in a scene, then even further up it was painted a darker colour. On the side walls it was painted white with abstract art on it. Just like the walls inside with their colourful abstract art on the walls, even the bar was red and black.

She felt it was like a div unlike D.B.A Club which had a lot of dark wood paneling on the walls and ceiling and a vivid blue long bar and tables along the wall opposite the bar. Then further in tables and chairs in front of a dance floor with colourful large stage. She preferred D.B.A place, it's outside was painted mauve. So this was what the colourful music scene here was like very vivid unlike any where else.

In this place she felt uneasy, besides giving her a headache from all the conflicting colours she decided to leave, and was about to turn around to leave just as a middle age pot belled red bearded man with a bandanna around his long grease red hair came up dressed in patched dungarees and colourful shirt.

Can I help you pretty girl, he said in a slimy way, putting his hand on her butt?

She so wanted to kick him in his balls as she pulled away. But instead said I wondering if you would be interest in taking me on as a solo singer for one or two nights. Hoping he'd say no as he was a creep and smelt of sweat fags and beer, his beard had fag dust in it. She took a step back.

As he circled her with a pleasing look on his face he licked his lips, then replied you could wait on tables with food, i'm sure you'd go down well with the male customers as he ran his hand on her butt again and pinched it.

If it hadn't been for the fact she needed the work in the bars, she'd have punch his manhood. No thanks as I'm a singer and piano player and if you pop into the D.B.A Club Friday at ten you'r hear me? Turned to walk out.

So you think you can sing girly. Then go give us a song on the piano. I don't buy without first trying it out running his hand again over her butt.

Again she wanted to punch this slime ball in the mouth but instead walked up to the stage, then stepped up on it and sat at a beer stained smelly piano which had its lid up. And started to play. She was surprised to find it sounded okay as she began to sing. Every one in the place stopped what they were doing and listened to her. She only sang one of the songs she knew as she wanted to get out of that place.

Suddenly every one started clapping her. And the slime ball greasy man smiled, so you really can sing girl. I'm sure the punters will love you. So what nights are you free?

Summer thought for a second about whether to say no or play there, after all it was money and she needed more gigs so she could rent somewhere.

Thursday and Friday and Saturday.I'm playing at 10 the first two so before or afterwards?

Friday and Saturday at midnight till one, and about payment we send a beer mug around the punters after each performance so depend on how much they like you, that's how much you get. I don't need to take a share of it. I make my money on drink sales and food, I believe other place's take a share. So pretty girl see you this Friday Midnight. Shake on it as he grabbed her hand and pulled her close to him. God you smell as good as you look baby.

God she wished he did as well. She stuck her nails into the palm of his hand as he was about to put his hand up inside her top, pulled herself away and turned and walked towards the door, see you Friday she said as she walked out in to the fresh air and wanted to scream but instead walked back to the guest house and Madam.

CHAPTER 3

Summers walked in to the Guest house bar ready for what ever Madam had to say to her, as it couldn't be worse than the slime ball.

Leaning up against the bar with a cocktail in her hand Madam was talking to a short thin shaven head black man. On seeing her, she glared angrily at her then beckoned her over.

Summer took out the rest of her roll and started to eat it as she walked over to the bar where you could help yourself to coffee in a paper cup and got herself one before going and sitting at a table right near them, much to Madams displeasure. She hoped to show Madam that she was a customer not employer.

She knew she was new to this grown up world of their's, but I am learning quickly. And I believe she can't order me about. I'm the guest here.

Madam not moving from the bar, spoke loudly to Summer, where the hell were you all day?

As you knew I wished to talk to you about your musical career here. This here is Wyatt, he's been waiting quit a while to hear you sing. As he has a vacant spot Friday night at 9. So when you've finished eating that thing, show him he's not wasting his time.

Not happy to be ordered about by Madam or any one, not even for another gig. Took a big bite then put the half eaton roll down took a gulp of coffee and got up. Dragged herself to the stage and sat at the piano, thought about what to play before she started then sang a song for 10 minutes. Turned on the piano stool and looked at them and waited for the verdict?

Mr Wyatt spoke first, not bad girl I'm sure I can use you at my place. I'v just told Madam the details.

And as I had to wait for you, I'm now late for another appointment. He then got up kissed Madams hand and left.

We'll girl you have a regular spot twice a week at the Fat Cat music club in the best street in the French quarter "Bourbon Street, what do you say to that?

I can't do 9 on Friday or after as I have two gigs, or Saturday as I also have the same again. It felt good saying no. She'd not used that word at home or school so it was a new word she'd use as much as she wanted. Got off the stage retrieved her roll and coffee and went up to sit on her Balcony and watch the people go by.

Madam sat fuming then picked up her phone and dialled Wyatt to see if there were other times Summer could sing.

After a while Wyatt came back with 12 30 midnight, as I'm sure she will be free then. Let me know as soon as, and switch off?

Madam told the assistant barman to go up and tell Summer she needed to talk to her as soon as.

It was nice sitting among all the flowering plants on the balcony. The noise of the Street didn't even worry her as she thought about the 3 gigs she had with BMC Balcony music club. Only they were all on the same days as the others. She'd have to juggle with the times so as not to be late she thought. As a voice behind her said Madam wants to speak to you now Miss "sorry" as he rushed back down stairs.

She thought about given it a miss and staying put. But decided to get it over with before she had to shower and change for her gig tonight in the bar down stairs. She dragged herself once again back down to the bar where Madam was waiting.

After a long talk between them, She agreed to do the gig's on different days to the others. Only because she hoped to earn enough in a couple of months to rent a room or flat some where. She had the diamonds she'd forgotten about with all that had happened. Tomorrow she'd see if she could sell a couple of them. Walked back up to her room and the balcony and peace.

Madam she felt was not to pleased she'd got herself 4 gigs in 2 other clubs without her help. Madam had mentioned about managing her. She told Madam that's it was a no as she had the other 4 gigs. There was nothing Madam could say or could do about it.

Summer sat thinking about what had just happened.The barman had mentioned that first night that she should be careful as Madam is looking to manage someone like herself. Summer had now told Madam that she was happy doing it herself. Which did not please Madam, she saw a side of Madam that was unpleasant. She wasn't happy that In half an hour she'd have to get ready for tonight performance down stair something she wasn't looking forward to.

As she soaked in the bath she reflected back on the last two days. Was it only 2 days, seemed like she'd been here longer. New Orleans she noticed had a mix of people, some nice some not so nice. She had thought Madam was nice at first but just like a lot of adults, unless they get what they want they turn nasty, and she wondered why some men were so lecherous, were men in other Cities like that?

On her walk around the City the last two days she had noticed a kick boxing club in Marigny, realising if she was to survive the place she would have to learn to take care of herself. So tomorrow she'd see if girls could join up and train. She valued never to be a victim ever again know matter what it took on her part.

Sitting at the piano that evening, the place was packed for 8 pm Thursday. She could see Madam walking around among the customers being queen bee as the barmen called her behind her back. Summer started to play a Jazz piece and decided to continued with Jazz for the whole hour.

She lost herself in her music as she always did, but she still had a bad taste in her mouth after the set to with Madam earlier. What had started as proprietor and guest at first, then she thought that they had become friends as well in a short time. How wrong could she be. Once she'd finished playing her mind went back to her thoughts on Madam, and wondered what share of tonight performance money she'd get. As it will go straight into a pot for a deposit on a place of her own so she could get out of that place.

She went to get off the stage when the singer of the next band stood in front of her baring her way. Baby stay as you play a mean piano, and we could do with you tonight? It's soul music some I'm sure you know, by the way I'm Orion Marshall you are?

Summer Dalla-Rosa and I'd like to stay and play piano thank you.
She had know problem with the songs as she knew them all and had played some of them at home when she was on her own on the grand piano she loved soul music.

It was a long night with a couple of short breaks where the band drank spirit, quite a lot of it. She had a problem excusing herself each time there was a round of drinks. She'd have to find a reason for not drinking spirit or beer and wine. As she sat on a bar stool and watch everyone getting plastered. How the band could play that way she never knew. As she needed a clear head.

She tried hard to think of a reason not to drink, over the noise of the customers. She could say buddhism again to this band. Her cross was now outside her blouse, as she fondled the cross around her neck then quickly put it in side of her top hoping know one noticed it. As Catholic drink, Moslem don't she didn't fancy that, Hindi no she didn't fancy it. It seemed there was only one Buddhist, and there was a buddhist shine outside the city with monks living there. When she looks up New Orleans on line, she had read there were a lot of Vietnams living on the edge of there and had bought their religion with them, yes Buddhist, the next person that try's to give her a drink that's what she'll say. And to make it more real she'd go visit the shine, also their open air market soon.

Summer stood waiting to get payed as the band packed up and Madam saw the customers out with her doorman it was 2 am. Summer was tired as it had been a long day but a good one.

Madam had already collected the money from the large beer mug before closing up.
Orion walked over to Madam, and said some words and looked towards Summer. Madam gave him her share of the money as well.

Summer decided to walk over and get hers instead of waiting for him to give it to her. And as they were talking about her why not, maybe she'd hear some of what they were saying. Orion was saying that the evening was good music wise, and even better with having Summer singing don't you think Madam?

Summer stood in front of them and interrupted them asking Can I have my share of tonights earnings please as I'm tired and would like to go to bed? Also as I'v already paid for my board I'd like the money you owe me for my solo gig Madam.
Need someone to undress you baby and tuck you in bed, Orion had a big smile on his face as he

spoke, as he handed her some notes and loose change.

Madam took no notice of Orion and put the rest of the money in her own pocket. Turned and looked at Summer, then reluctantly handed some notes from another pocket and handed it to her dropping some notes on the floor as she did so. Then she walked away into the interior of the place not saying a word.

Summer bent and picked up the notes and walked back up stairs to her room without answering Orion, before counting the money she'd made singing.

There had been a full house that evening and spending on drink seemed good as she dropped the money on the bed and sat. Looked at the collection of one and five dollar notes laying there with several dollar coins, it didn't look to bad for the night's 2 gig. Picked up the coins and counted 9 dollars then the notes, and as she counted there were two 20 dollar notes included. In all she had seventy dollars for a six hour stint with two ten minutes breaks. She'd know Idea if that was good, she'd have to wait till the other gigs and see what she got for each of them. One thing she realised was that she'd have to sell a couple of the diamonds tomorrow sooner than she'd hoped. She couldn't stay where she was being manipulated. Also she'd inquire about kickboxing lessons as well tomorrow while in that part of town.

Now she needed to sleep as she'd been up around 18 hours and was really tired but pleased that she had got herself a lot of gigs at the start of her new life. She heard a catching at the door it was the old cat as she opened it she shot in and onto Summers bed. You want some food opening a tin of tuna and put the tin on the floor. Got her self undressed cleaned her teeth and washed her face, walked back into her bedroom and the old cat was curled up on her bed. Okay I don't mind sharing with you.

After a couple of week's working hard at different clubs, she managed to save a good bit. Even managed to get 200 dollars for two smaller diamonds. She went on line to see what they went for, it was a bit more than she'd got. But knew she couldn't ask the full price as she'd stolen them. She added the money to her pile of notes, pleased with herself as she would soon have enough to rent a cheap place for a while.

Madam was giving her the cold shoulder now, not that she minded. She still needed to play there twice a week, although she believed Madam was dipping into their money during the evening before giving it to the band and herself.

Now she was off to her kickboxing session with Billy boy her coach, a thickset black man with dreadlocks tied back in a pony tail. He was shorted than herself at around five foot seven or eight with muscles like Arnold Schwarzenegger.

Summer had them three times a week, as New Orlean was full of randy men. The proprietor of the HI HO Lounge was no exception as she found out after her first gig there. She'd had to punch him in the balls to stop him groping her breasted. Summer thought he'd sack her but instead pretended it never happened, much to her surprise

Summer's birthday was in two days May seventh a Wednesday. She had one gig that evening in the Blue Moon Saloon in Lafayette Convent Street, a two hour section but good money. Only it was a long walk back to Marigny, she didn't want to spent good money on a taxi when she had two good feet. Only after her first gig last Wednesday she found walking back to Marigny a drunk tried it on with her then a group of white youth also. She'd barely got away with a torn blouse and she lost a good earring one of a pair she was fond of.

So for this Thursday's gig she'd bought herself a flick knife in "Junk Above" in D'Hemecourt Street. Ask the proprietor straight out if he had any flick knives as she'd heard from one of the bar men at the Balcony Music club that you might. I'm staying there as well as singing. She hoped he trust her more if she said all that, as she knew it was illegal to sell or have one on your person. But it worked she got one, there was a good selection and chose one about six inches unopened and had a beautiful carved hilt.

Summer hated being touched because of her stepfather, and until she could physical defend her self with her fist and feet the knife would be the next best thing. Whether she'd use it she had know Idea, as she found her whole being changed when she was just touch let along sexual. Her stepfather was to blame for that. God she'd not thought about him or her mother in the four weeks she'd been there, so quickly put them out of her mind.

The session had been good, but she felt she had a long way to go before she could really defend her self. Walked back though Washington Square Park. And along to a good take away she'd used before and bought Muffet full of different meat, cheese with a topping of mixed pickles, it was the size of a dinner plate so would do two meals, and at five dollars it was cheap.

As she walked along holding it away from her in it's rapping, the grease was dripping down on the ground and her hand was cover in grease so she was glad to see the guest house come music venue in sight. Hoping Madam would be preoccupied some where else.

Up in her room she put the muffet on a plate and washed her hands made a coffee and sat and eat half and put the other have in a plastic bag for tomorrow and went and had a soak in the tub before getting ready for her gig later that night. The cat was a sleep on her bed so she fed it after her bath.

It was quarter past one and she had enjoyed her session at the lounge as she started her walked back to the guest house. She even got a bit more money than her first session there last week as word had got around and the place was full.

The side Streets wern't well lite as she walked along clutching her knife in her right hand beside her. Walking through Washington Park she heard foot steps behind her so slowed down and waited for the person to pass. Which he quickly did then disappeared from sight, she gave a sye of relief and quickened her pass, then suddenly out from the shadows a figure jumped out and grabbed her from behind around the waist, the park was dimly lite and she was near some shrubbery so it was even darker so she wouldn't be able to see him.

A voice said saw you baby singing this evening, thought you were good, as well as looking good. You smell even better baby as he ran his face over her hair. God I want to fuck you baby.

All this time her heart was racing and she was as mad as hell. She was fed up with guys thinking she was an easy lay, a Word she'd heard on TV. Her whole body was getting hotter and hotter till she could contain her self any more, lifted her hand up high above her, as his hand went to go between her legs. She bought it down on to what she believed to be his neck and stuck the knife into the flesh.

He gave out a scream and pulled away from her. Summer turned around to face him. She was not going to be treated like a bitch in heat, holding the bloody knife in her blood stained hand she realised she'd gone in to the side of his neck right next to his ear. Blood had started to gush from the wound.

He suddenly lurched forward at her with his blood stained hand. You bastard look what you done you cow, as he held his left hand over his now blood dripping neck. Then lunged forward I'll kill you for that as he went to try and strangle her. Summer without hesitation plugged the knife back into him, straight into his heart and stepped back as blood burst out of his chest before he fell to the ground.

Summer stood looked at his dead body, you won't be rapping anyone else now, so who's the bastard now? Then bent wiped the knife on him and her hands and turned and walked on till she came to the park gates, turned looked back smiled and said serves you right and walked on back to the guest house.

She had felt nothing by what she had done as she walked back into the now empty guest house bar through the side door and up to her room, and straight into the bathroom to wash the blood off and saw her blouse was cover as well. She'd have to soak it in salt cold water while she sleep. The whole experience had left her cold. There was no way she could destroy the blouse. She liked that blouse, and lots of people knew it belonged to her. So she did just that in the handbasin. And watched the water turning bloody as she smiled to her self, changed and got in to bed to sleep. It had been a good night she'd earned good money still smiling to her self before falling into a peaceful sleep with the cat curled beside her.

The dead body in the park was on the TV news that morning as she sat at the bar and had a coffee and listened to the barmen degaussing it with Madam. Then Madam turned to her, you should have someone accompanying you late at night after gigs as that could have been you?

Summer sipped her coffee and then spoke. I'll be fine really. I'm sure it doesn't happen to ofter.

One of the barmen Jason told her that in some places in New Orleans "not all" I'm afraid it does. I'm sure one of the guys here would pick you up in the car after work and drive you back here for a small fee.

Every bloody thing here seem's to be money related she said to them at the bar. I told you I can take care of my bloody self but thankyou. Now I'm off for a jog. Leaving them to carry on talking about the murder and herself. Funny the guy was attacked around the time she walked through the park, she'd not noticed any one on her way back.

That night she had the first of the two gigs that she had got herself the second day in the City, first HI HO Lounge at nine then D.B.A Club at midnight. She'd carry her knife around with her tonight after that man was murdered and they haven't for him. She'd also take the knife were ever she went except the kickboxing Club.

Both Gigs wen't fine as did the walk back later that night. And for the next couple of weeks all was fine. Then one Saturday morning over coffee Jason who she'd found out was Madam's son and barman told her that he had heard that the proprietor of One Eyed Jacks in the French Quarter heard her sing last night here at the Balcony music club. And He'd heard Madam arrange a deal with him for her to play there. She's going to disguise it any minute now. I know how you feel about being managed so thought I should tell you.

Thanks Jason for telling me. I'll be off before Madam appears. Bent and kissed him on the cheek and quickly walked out of the Bar. What Jason hadn't told her was that his father had left the place to him when he died. And that when he reached twenty-three he would inherit the place. Something Madam was not happy about, so was trying to make as much money as she could before hand. And that was in six years times"

Once outside she decided to go to that Club after her jog to see what kind of place it was. And if she liked it then go back that afternoon and introduce herself. And see if he would be interested in hiring her with know strings attached, like Madam?

One Eyed Jacks was on Toulouse, where most of the building had balconies and side entrances as she looked though the wrought iron high gate in to the side entrance she saw through to a nice French courtyard. Then Looked through the window of the Bar, it looked very French Bohemian unlike the others she sung at. She wondered what musical acts played there. She liked the look of the place, and liked the Idea of playing there if the money was good. As she could not keep staying at the Guest house for much longer as life around madam have become intolerable. She'd come back later when it opened around four pm. For now she'd talk to Madam which she wasn't looking forward to.

Things had not gone well with Madam, after she'd told her she was going to see if she could get her own gigs there. Putting Madam straight about the fact she had come to New Orleans to make it on her own with her musical career without Madams help.

Madam tried to explain that she could get her on the international circuit in Europe with her voice. With Summers talent and her know how and contact's, they could take the continent and States by storm. So what did she think?

Summer didn't need to thing twice about it. She just said three words "no thankyou" And left Madam fuming to go up and changed before going back out. This time to sell two more diamonds and then go and find a Realtor agent to see if she can find a cheap rental, as she believed she had enough money from the gigs over the month, and with a couple more diamonds she'd and her saving. She would need the money from two more gig to live on after she'd moved out.

Now the money for her room in the guest house was due for another month there. So she decided to just paid for one more week that morning. Summer didn't want to have to pay Madam for the whole month's rent, as it would mean she couldn't move out yet. Not that Madam took it too well only getting one weeks rent, as she knew she was earning good money now from several gigs.

Summer left the Balcony bar and Guest house and walked towards St Claude Avenue, she had looked up Realtors then phoned one to see if they had anything on there books for 900 dollars a months rent? She felt she could afford that for now.

The agent had a couple, one was in Marigny a two bedroom wooden Creole house with balcony, small back yard. It had a small lounge and kitchen also a bathroom renewed that year. 800 dollars a month, with two months up front. It is fully furnished she told her with all new furniture and furnishings. Summer liked where it was as it was situated on St Claude Avenue which run all the way along and connecting to the Bywater District and beyond, it was a very long road of about three miles. To the left it went all the way to Esplanade Avenue where she could walk easily to, then cross Esplanade in to the French Quarter. She'd not even seen it yet but she liked what she'd heard. And was now on her way to do just that.

The Realtor greeted her and showed her around. It was small but had every thing she needed and a bonus box room come single bedroom. It was big enough for her to put a second hand piano in the sitting room, she'd seen two in the pawn brokers where she had bought her knife.

The Realtor asked what she thought of the place, as it had just come on the market only three days, and won't be on for long at that price with the refit?

Summer didn't hesitate and said I'll take it. So back to the Realtor office to fill out form's and pay a deposit holding fee and one months rent.

Summer nearly lost it as she payed the sixteen hundred dollars in cash. As it should have been a bankers draught. Summer explained she didn't have a bank account. Much to the Realtor dismay. But after a lot of talking and a visit to the near by bank that they used, so she could open an account to prove she was kosher. Summer got the house. It took over three hours. But it was worth it.

Now before collecting her luggage from the guest house she'd go to see if she could get a couple more gigs at One-Eyed-Jacks. As she was a short distance to Toulouse Street. Now she had rent to pay she needed all the work she could get. Funny the realtor was suspicious of cash.

It seemed adults have to have plastic whether it be visa or credit card. But luckily she had taken all her savings with her and her birth certificate as well as her I D, so it was no problem and opening up her first Bank account, which in a way was a good thing as she could deposit her earnings every morning after the night before gigs instead of having money in the house.

She was deep in thought and nearly got hit by a slow moving car in narrow Toulouse. And found herself as she jumping out of the way in between two parked cars carrying her groceries, she was right outside the very Club. She was glad the streets of the French District were only one lane or the food might have been all over the street as she walked inside the Club.

The place was more oh less the same layout, stage at the back as the others. Only the decor was different. Still colourful but different. Less sleazy, as it was in the Quarter with its shops art gallery and restaurant's and a Grocer's near bye where she couldn't resit buying food before checking out the Club.

As she continued looking around a bohemian dressed middle age thick set clean shaven bald man stopped her in her tracks and asked her what she was doing noising around without a drink so early in the evening and with baggage?

Summer was about the same height as him as she busted out, I'm hoping you will hire me to sing and play piano. I have been told I play a mean piano. I'm called the new Mississippi song bird.

Sorry I didn't recognise you from last night. So Madam sent you, I thought she would be with you?

Madam was only my landlady nothing more. If you would like I can play a tune for you.

Know need miss your hired, two gigs a week, so now let's finalise the times and days you're work. Oh my name is Napoleon Jones an unconventional name like my place. As for payment we have a cover charge to enter here twelve dollars per person so each night will be different, as it's down to how many come in to how much you get paid. And a share of drinks money.

Summer didn't mind as long as she got her fair share, she told him as they sat and disguised the days and time's of her gigs. Before she was off to get her things from Madams place and move into her new house.

Back at Balcony Bar, the place was filling up as she managed to get to her room unseen and out with her luggage and groceries. She was in high spirit as she turned and looked back at the place, remembering how she had felt when she first saw it all lite up and covered in plants and thought what a great looking place.

Now she was pleased to be off to her first home on her own terms. Turned and walked around the corner out of Royal Street and further into Marigny. Which was more a residential area where working class people lived. Although most residence had a love of life music and festivals, she realised to live anywhere in New Orleans meant you were unconventional or you wouldn't live there. Like her self.

St Claude residence were mostly all home as it was dinner time, either eating or watching the news as she stopped out side 224 her new home. The couple next door were sitting out on their Veranda on that warm May barmy evening, the smell of rich spices mixed with blossom was a little sickly as she walked up the steps to her Veranda then front door, and put her luggage down and took out the key excited at the thought of moving in.

A voice came from one of the 2 people next door welcoming her, and introducing them selves Jules and Sayde. She gave her own name Summer. And a large friendly looking coloured woman dressed in a colourful dress asked her if she'd like some food as they had plenty.

Summer smiled opened her door picked up the luggage and groceries turned and thanked them kindly and said she would eat later after she'd settled in.

Another large round faced coloured woman dressed in a below knee length brightly colour dress and slip-on shoes came from there front door carrying a tray of food on seeing Summer gave her a big smile, then replied she'd put some food in a plastic container and leave it on Summers veranda. She told her that she could easily heat it up in the microwave as she pleased.

Summer smiled in reply to both the women and the thin coloured man who was sitting at the out side table. And went inside put the bags down in the sitting room. There were no hallway in Creole houses she'd notice's that all rooms were small and off one another which she liked. It meant no one could sneak up on her or hide any where. Remembering her stepfather grabbing hold of her while she walked down their hall. This would never happen in her new place.

After half an hour she'd unpacked her things and put the food that she had bought in the kitchen. So she could now make herself a coffee. The kitchen was fully equipped making it easer for her, as she had know Idea what the kitchen needed. Went back in the sitting room and switched on the Television and sat content now. Then remembered the food outside her door and went and got it. She'd eat it later. Looked at her mobile phone it was eight thirty-five. She had a two hour gig at nine in One Eyed Jacks tonight, this would be her first Wednesday gig.

The gig was good and she was happy with a short break of an hour while another band played before she went back on this time with a backing band. Also that night the money had been good. The backing band guys had also asked her if she'd mind if they accompany her permanently as they were sure her playing piano alone in a noisy bar wasn't enough.

Summer didn't have to think twice, but told Bryan that she kept her name and his bands name was added on so they would be know as the Mississippi song bird and the jaybirds so they kept there separate identities. And instead of leaving at one in the morning, they sat as another band played the last hour. As she gave them all the bars and dates that she played. So only there gigs and new gigs would she sing with them. Then she asked them, if anyone know's of a hall they could rehearse in or a garage. Anywhere so they could go though her songs with them. They even disguised money, and after over an hour everything was ironed out, and she would see them at Adams parents garage with Bryan Paul and Shawn to rehearse. Then they all left the Club as it was about to close.

The night had gone well as she faced the long walk back to her place, though the Quarter towards Esplanade Avenue then up it till she came to Louis Armstrong Park and started walking through to her street. As she walked along she felt someone was following her, had been most of the way from the Club but she dismissed it. Her house was still a distance away as she quickened her pace. The Park was empty of people and her Street as they were all asleep in their home's as it was a Wednesday and well gone three am, and locals didn't go out clubbing till weekends. So her Street was no different it was empty and dark.

She knew It was Tourist that made the numbers up at the Clubs during the week, and stayed in B and B or hostels in the French District or around Frenchmen Street not where she lived so she was alone there, so pulled her knife out of her pocket just incase of trouble. A tall young man in a black hoody passed her, then walked out of view.

The street had a row of large tree's along both sides of the street same as a lot of major streets. Which looked nice but meant someone could hide behind them, so kept close to the houses fences away from the tree's along the road side.

Just as she thought he'd gone, a dark figure loomed out behind her and grabbed her from behind. And put his sweaty hand over her mouth dragging her through a gate, into what was a derelict building. Before she knew what was

48

happening to herself, a strange feeling started to come over her.

Summer realised she hadn't noticed the empty house in her street before, then something suddenly came over her just like the park where the other guy was killed. She'd not thought about that night till now.

Summer became a mad woman once again. Her body was not going to be violated by any one ever again. She became a wild beast, the knife ready in one hand with a sudden urge of strength she twisted her body out from his grip to his surprise. She was now facing him in the shadow of the derelict building.

Suddenly from the darkness of the empty house a large black rat ran out between their legs then another pass them and another making the guy shudder. Summer showed no syne that she even notice them. He froze for a second just as he was before to swing a fist in her face.

She used that second on his part and brought the knife up to his arm and cut into it before he could move his fist near her face.

He screamed out in pain grabbing his now bloody arm.

Summer as in a dream thrust the knife in his stomach and sliced it up to his navel and stepped back as his blood spurted out of the large wound.

She couldn't make out his face too well what with the hood over his head and the shadow from the building as a frail voice said why? There was no need for any of this. I only wanted to fuck you. Done it many times before without all this. Now I'm goner have to kill you, something I didn't want to do pulling a knife out of his belt. Only before he could use it she slit his throat.

He grabbed his bloody neck and stomach with both hands as he now lay on the ground as the rats came back into the front yard with the smell of blood and waited in the shadows for her to leave before they started to tuck into his flesh as he lay dyeing. without a thought she calmly wiped her knife on his good arm then put it back in her pocket turned and walked away back out onto the Street as the rats rushed forward as she walked away, she could now hear his screams as she got near her home as if nothing had happened.

Next morning she went for her usual run alone Riverwalk. Last night's incident never even entered her head, it was as if it never happened. If she had remembered In any case she knew murder was not new to New Orleans. Far from it as it was known as one of the murder capitals of America. Earlier She'd watched the news that morning on the television, it didn't even bother to even cover it if she'd even remembered it.

Now back from her run she decided to go grocery shopping to fill up her cupboard's fully. Smiling to her self under the shower she said aloud I'm going to buy all the things that my bitch of a mother said were bad for me. If they could see me now happily fending only too well on my own. I wonder if they are happy now they don't have to worry about me any more. My life couldn't be better.

CHAPTER 4

Summer had been in New Orleans just over 8 weeks. And life was good they had even changed the name for the backing Band again. The Eagle's, she was pleased to add it on to Mississippi song bird and the Eagle's on the boards. And the new sound was even better, giving them a good following now and a couple more new gigs.

Jason had been hanging out at One Eyed Jacks place when she and the Band played. Much against his Mothers wishing, as she expected him to be behind the bar full time.

Only since he meet Summer and they becoming friends, he had started to say no to his mother. She'd tell him constantly why would she be interested in a four eyed skinny ugly looking guy like you, if it wern't for the guesthouse Club you own stupid boy.

You're mean mother, you know nothing about us. We are just good friends something you would know nothing about seeing you don't have any slamming the bar door as he walked out, off to hear her sing. He was not going to let the mean cow get under his skin as he walked to his car, he couldn't wait till he was twenty-three, because then he would give the old witch her marching orders smiling to himself.

Summer was pleased to see him that Saturday evening at the D.B.A swanky Club. Out side the air was still hot that evening as it was now June and the days only got hotter and humid. "People spent the middle of the hot humid day's in doors now till October when it got cooler". In side the Club it had air conditioning unlike many of the other place's herself and the Band played at. Summer thought maybe the tourist would drop off as it heated up. But Jason told her that the hotels cut there prices by over half till October which brought the younger tourist there in droves as they were on collage vacation. And that Saturday was no exception as the Band at eleven started to play.

Money was still good even thou she had to now share with the four band members, as she shared out the money before her own solo Midnight gig there before going home with Jason that night.

It was nearly 1 30am as he drove back to Marigny. Jason was quiet as they drove along, windows down as they listened to the music from the other clubs still going including the D.B.A. Only her gig finished at 1pm.

Summer sensed there was something worrying him, so instead of staying for a short while at her place she was going to get him to stay longer hoping that he might confide in her as they had become quit close. Only near her home he started to chat on about everything else but his problem.

As they drew outside Summers home, she turned to him. Jason why don't you come in and stay a while longer not just for a coffee, maybe a snack the nights still young looking at her watch it was 1 forty-two am?

Thanks I was not looking forward to going back to my place yet.

Summer was glade he excepted, maybe she could get him to open up to her as they walked up the steps and indoors.

As she potted about in the tiny kitchen making coffee on her new machine she'd bought. Then got the muffuletta out of the fridge, that she'd bought earlier while jogging around the area of riverwalk. Summer got two plates and cut it in half as it was the size of a large dinner plate. Even cold it smelt good, full of cured meats provolone cheese, olive dressing with the two round bread roll. No pickle as that gave her gip.

Put them on the tray and went into the sitting room. Jason had turned the television on and was watching a late night horror film as she put it down on the coffee table. You will eat half of the muffuletta, as I got a whole one so I could share with you?

Jason smile so you knew I'd be staying picking his half up thanks Summer taking a big bite into it?

Now Jason please talk to me, something is on your mind. I noticed on my break you were quiet, not a bit like you.

It's my Mother again, today when she gave out the monthly cash in hand wages. She did it again, my money was short. This has gone on only since you left. I spoke to her about it and she was cruel with her words again. I can't wait to take over ownership, but that's along way off yet. A body can't manage on what she pays me I'm going to have to find a part time job to make ends meet. It wouldn't be so bad if I could have free meals in "my own restaurant" but I have to pay like the rest except her. I'v tried talking to the solicitor but know joy there as mother is the executor of the bar till I am twenty-three. In two months I'm twenty-one so it's two more years of her bleeding the bar and guesthouse dry I'm sure of it.

When Father became too ill to run the Balcony bar she then took over as I was only fourteen. But when he died he left it to me not her because she was also a cow to him at the end.

I can't go on like I am. But I have know Idea what I can do about it?

Summer's heart suddenly became cold and her thoughts black as she felt numb. She knew just what to do about Madam, a wicked smile on her face. Poor Jason I'm sure things will get better soon for you, you see.

How can you say that, you know what she's like, she can make my life hell? And as I said I have two more years of her. Is there something you know that I don't?

As you know I'm a buddhist and believe good will out. Meaning the wrong one does come's back on oneself. So give it time.

If you say so you haven't made me feel any better thou, but I'm sure you mean well. No good asking you for a whisky or even a beer as you're a buddhist. I'll have to make do with another coffee? As he sat and started to dossed off.

Morning came and she'd slept like a log as she got out of bed and stretched and walked over to the window to pulled back the curtains. The view was depressing as she kept promising to see to the backyard. Oh we'll maybe later as she looked at her watch it was 9 34 am. The air conditioning made the place feel cool inside, but she knew once outside on her jog it would be very warm even this early. Put on her jogging gear and trainers got her water bottle and phone and was ready to go jogging as usual at that time. Walked back through the kitchen into the sitting room where Jason had spent the night asleep on the couch, she hadn't had the heart to wake him up. He looked like a little boy curled up sound asleep, Without his spec's he wasn't bad looking. She hoped he'd sleep at least another couple of hours, unlike herself who only needed six hours sleep a night. So silently walked to the front door and let herself out trying not wake him. She'd become fond of him, he was the only guy who hadn't tried it on.

The hot air hit her in the face after her cool home. The St Claude Avenue Street was empty as she jogged towards the end to Esplanade Avenue, which ran off North Peters Street along side the river then up to North Rampart Street and Louis

Armstrong Park just across Rampart. She'd sung at a jazz concert in the Park a couple of weeks earlier as she ran on down Esplanade, counting as she ran three Street off on the right till she came to Royal Street where the Balcony bar and guest house was.

By now the people had begun to appear on the Street, Office workers going to get the streetcar at the bottom of Esplanade or hospital works, as people from there worked in the clubs and bars and restaurants as well as the French market which was a large covered over the top place. A tourist market full of nicknack's and leather goods which didn't open till around ten. Summer stood on the corner of Royal and watched the few people hurrying to there work and was glad she'd never have to do a normal job like them. Although New Orleans was mostly a tourist place not really a place of big business unlike most Cities else where. She smiled to her self as she said good morning to a lady carrying two coffee beakers as she hurried pass to catch the Streetcar.

Now for the guest house she told herself as she started walking towards it. The Street was empty around that area, only the local cats were about. Summer saw a familiar black Cat old Maggie, who on seeing her ran straight up to her. I see Madam still under feeds you poor thing, I'm afraid I don't have any tin tuna this time bending and rubbing Maggie behind the ear.

The cat remembered Summers kindness with tuna and rubbed herself around Summers legs as she walked up the stairs to the bar's large old heavy doors which opened with a large key. The key it self if she remembers was very large and ornate making the keyhole large taking out a hair pin from her hair. Maggie had joined her and stood as if she knew what she was up to. Summer smile at the cat wish me luck puss.

To Summers surprise she heard the click from the large lock, puss we are in as she pushed one of the doors open. The smell of stale beer and sweat hit her. Took out her hankie from her pocket and put it over her face. You would think Maggie I'd be use to the smell by now. Entered and quickly hurried throw the bar area to the side door and though into the guesthouse stairs followed by Maggie. Then up them. And along the corridor to Madams door where she stoped as she could hear music in the distance from inside. I have a feeling old girl that Madam is soaking in her bubble bath as usual at this time, looking at her watch.

Summer silently opened the door and walked into Madams room. As she opened the door the smell of cheap perfume mixed with sweat was sickly. She'd walked into what looked like a french boudoir with it's pink lace shawls covering the lampshade's, and king size wrought iron bed with its pink satin sheets and several large pink silk pillows. Hanging over the wrought iron posted were several strands of cheap beads. The whole room looked and smelt cheap and nasty she felt as she looked around, more like a nocking shop she felt as she walked over to the bathroom's open door. Madam had her eyes closed as she looked in to a very old large green bathroom sweet and floor to ceiling green wall tiles. Horrid she thought, it looked as if it hadn't been updated in a very long time.

Just then Madam opened her eyes and lifted a hand from the pink bubbles and picked up a full wine glass that sat on the side of the bath, a wine bottle stood on the floor beside it.

Summer quickly noticed the music was coming from an old brown electric Radio balanced on the side of the bath, it was plugged into a sock near the bath.

Madam suddenly saw her, and shouted what the fuck you doing here Summer. Thought you'd had enough of this place now you're famous. Madam then noticed Maggie, and got a soaking wet sponge from the bubbles and throw it at Maggie, bloody cat get out. Only it missed as she jumped in front of Summer. Both of you get out before I call Jason to throw you out.

Summer smiles knowing full well Jason was asleep on her coach, evidently Madam didn't know he hadn't come home, Summer realised as she ran her fingers over the precariously hung Electric Radio. And said nothing.

What the fuck do you want standing there with that bloody cat, who by now was sitting on the edge of the bath at the bottom her yellow eyes pierced throw Madam as if she knew what Summer was about to do.

Getting agitated Madam shouted out what do you want with me?

I want you to die of course smiling, tipping the Radio into the bath. Turned and walked over to the door, turned and looked back to see Madam's face disappear under the bubbles her feet now up in the air at the other end of the bath while water poured over it. She turned and kept walking till she was out on the Street not passing anyone on the way, and kept walking till she came to Esplanade stopping for a minute to buy a newspaper. Maggie was now standing beside her, the old girl had followed her all the way there. Summer bent and picked her up, you want to come live with me. Maggie purred and put her head into Summers chest. Okay lets go home have breakfast.

Back outside her house people were now sitting on their verandas drinking coffee reading newspapers as she walked along. She said good morning to her next door neighbour's as she climb her steps and opened her front door. As she

57

stepped inside, she saw that Jason was still fast asleep. Her wall clock said nearly 11 as she put the cat down on the sitting room rug. Walked into the kitchen got Maggie her tuna and a dish of milk. Before getting her self a coffee and a dish of cereal, went and sat out on the veranda to eat it, feeling happy that all's right with the world now.

Maggie stood in the kitchen enjoying her first decent meal in a while. Before going into Summers bedroom and jumped up on the unmade bed and curled up and went to sleep, something she'd not done since Summer had moved out of the guest house, she knew now she was home.

Summer was enjoying the morning sun, when Jason came outside in his boxer shorts looking for her. Girl you let me over sleep it's gone 11, what were you thinking? You know how my mother gets if I haven't seen that the staff do their jobs before the bar opens at lunch time.

I'm sure It want hurt for once to be late, i'm sure the staff have done it a thousand times so no what's what any way Jason. Get you a coffee while you shower as you smell. I myself haven't been up long, jogged to buy a newspaper.

Jason turned not saying anything and went in and showered. He was not looking forward to the roff of his mother, it was all right for Summer she didn't have to live there now. Got dressed then noticed a cat sound asleep on Summers bed. Then shock his head maybe he'd just not noticed before. Just then his phone went it was Elio at the bar asking him to return straight away, as something had happened to Madam.

Jason didn't ask just quickly got dressed, as he knew his mother was now on the rampage as he wasn't there when she got up. God I hate that woman. Walked out to tell Summer saying my master summons me via Elio the barman on the phone. If I can I'll see you tonight at your gig God will.

I'm sure it will be fine, stick up for your self. Tell her you're a grown man with a life of your own, and that from now on you are only working 7 hours for a far wage. Sound as if you mean it. You will be surprised to see her reaction you see Jason. Bent and kissed his forehead. Before he gave her a look of disbelieve, and quickly hurried off in his car toward his mothers street not saying a word in reply.

As Jason turned in to his street he could see an Ambulance and a couple of police cars out side the Music Club. Now what he thought?

Walked up to the Bar, as a police woman came out of the bar. As Jason went to walk in pass her.

You can't go in there sir looking at him.

I live here what has happened, where is my mother?

You'd better come inside and sit down. I'll get the Sergeant to talk to you. A large thick set man in uniform came from the back and came over to Jason. May I ask who you are young man?

This is my place, and my mother manages it for me. Where is she? Has something happened to her. Was there a robbery, I keep telling her not to keep so much money in the place.

No son, I'm afraid there has been an accident your mother is dead.

What, How?

She was Electrocuted in the bath by her radio I'm afraid. Looks as if she balanced it on the side of the bath stretched for her wine bottle by the bath and knocked the radio in to the bath. I'm so sorry. Is there someone you can call to be with you at a time like this as you don't want to be alone?

I have this place to get ready for lunch time customers, mother wouldn't want me to close the place for any reason not even her death. And yes I have someone I can call, thinking of Summer.

The police sergeant just looked at Jason, as there was nothing else to say and turned and walked out of the Bar his work was done there.

Jason was in shock as he couldn't believe he was free of the old witch but not this way. Got up and started organised the staff to get on with opening the place, as it would have been his mothers wish. From now on he told them he was in charge and things will be a lot different from now on.

Took out his mobile phone and phoned Summer, he knew he should phone the solicitor but wanted time to think. And find out where he stood with the Bar with another solicitor before contacting him. As he believed mother was letting the solicitor fuck her to keep him sweet where her managing the Bar was concerned.That word death and mother he couldn't believe it still. Dailed Summers number his hand was shaking as he held the phone and waited to hear her voice. Then blurted it all out without taking a breath.

Summer could not believe it, after all she'd said that morning to Jason. I'll be straight around, poor thing you must be distressed?

No Summer I don't feel anything. Maybe it hasn't hit me yet. I'll get off the phone so you can come now please?

Summer walked to the bar with a heavy heart, much as she disliked the woman, she wouldn't wish her dead. As her thought turned to Jason, he'll have to take care of his mothers funeral and business, at least I can try and be there for him. God it was hot as she neared the Bar, she was sure you could fry an egg on the pavement.

Dam she suddenly remember Maggie asleep in her house. How the hell did Madams cat get into my house, oh well she's here now only what if she needed to go to toilet, fuck it. Nothing she could do about it now as she walked up the steps into the bar. Must remember before going home to find a pet shop and buy cat litter and tray she said aloud just as Jason spotted her and came over.

Hi Summer I have been organising the staff for the day, now you're here I'll go on line and find an honest solicitor if there is one in New Orleans? Want a drink of some kind before we start.

An ice cold Coke would be nice Jason? Jason asked Cheryl if she'd get one and bring it into the office with a cold beer thanks. A word his mother never used, but from now on he would he told her as they entered his mothers office.

Jason ran his hands over the back of his mothers red leather swivel chair, then sat in it. It felt good as he switched on the Computer and realised he didn't know the password. Summer I can't unlock the computer to get the bar files or find a solicitor what the fuck will I do.

Don't panic, go on your sell phone or tablet to find the solicitor then you can go though all the words or numbers your mother might use as a password. I'm sure we'll find it.

Found one the name is Steeg Law firm LLC, now to phone them wish me luck. After 20 minutes in conversation on the phone Jason had an appointment for 4 pm that very afternoon.

There you go Jason that was easy no? Now for passwords, would she use her date of birth like I have?

I'll try only I don't know her real age?

Don't worry it will be on her ID card Jason. After a few minutes looking for it Jason put the numbers in the computer and it worked straight away. You're a genies Summer. Now for the bar and guest house documents.

Summer pulled up a chair beside Jason as they started going though the files. After several hours and taking copies of the ones relevant to Jason and his ownership of the place and pulled the accounts of both business's he was ready for the solicitor. Thanks for being with me, you will come with me to the solicitors. But first we'll go and have dinner in "my Restaurant" god that sounded good on the tongue smiling at her.

I told the staff that when they take their 30 minute break in stead of 15, they can go in the Restaurant and have a free meal. Things are going to be better around here. And by the accounts the place was doing great. There is a good amount of money in my mothers account as well as the business account. I'm going to increase the staffs wages when all this is settled by the solicitor.

By the time Summer was due to go and sing at D.B.A Club at 9 all had been straighten out by the solicitor, who had set up an interview with his mothers solicitor to straighten it all out. The place was and is Jason. And although he was a miner when his father died once he became 18 he could have taken control of the business as there was no executive documents that I can find that say your mother is in charge.

The solicitor told them we do things a little different down south, 18 is the age you become a man. You're going to have to get a death certificate and bury your mother before you can transfer the money in her account to yours.

Jason Walked on air after hearing all that the solicitor had said as Summer told him that she'd have to leave him as she had to go find a pet shop that was still open at 5 43pm then go and buy some groceries in Royal Street at the 10 a clock shop before going back to her place to get ready for her gig.

Jason hugged her and thanked her for being with him, explained he wouldn't be able to watch her sing as he now had a Bar to run. But I'll get one of the barmen to drive you, and thanks again.

Thats fine with me Jason I'll pop in tomorrow sometime, bent and kissed his sweaty brow "as it was still very hot and humid". At least the air conditions was still on at her place and in the club tonight as she smiled and walked out side to the car to find a Pet shop. She was sure she'd pass one when she went walking down Esplanade Avenue at the bottom, if they hurried in the car maybe it would still be open after all shops don't open till 10 in the morning.

Back at her place the cat greeted her, rubbing it self around her legs. Okay Maggie lets hope you didn't poo on any of the rugs or my bed, as she walked around looking. All seemed okay till she went in the toilet to go to pee and say a poo in the bath. Maggie had followed her looking pleased with herself. Thats not so bad old girl, but now you have a proper litter tray I'll set up in here for you before I sort out my clothes for tonights gig. Something thin to stop me sweating even with there old air conditioning at the Club. Maybe Jason will install it in his now god I hope so?

Summer had nearly an hour to spare before she had to be at the club, so she sat for half an hour on the veranda outside. The lady next door and a couple of ladies were out there with a fan going full blast while drinking what looked like Rum. They saw her and started to chat to her. Summer didn't mind and chatted back. Told them about her friends mother's accident. And how stupid to balance a radio on the side of the bath. Don't know if you knew her, she ran the Balcony bar and Guest house not far from here.

They hadn't but were sorry for Summers friend. Then talked about more pleasant things till she had to leave, as she went back inside to tell Maggie she would be back leaving water and dried cat food down before collecting her bag and left locking the door behind her.

Weeks passed and Summer had more gigs at Jasons place now he was the official owner. The funeral had been quite big with people parading though the streets with a marching coloured band. Jason had her cremated as they was no way he was having her buried just in case she floated up out of her burial site, he told people at the funeral as there was very little earth top soil in New Orleans as the ground was wetland. Jason did lay on a party after, more to celebrate the fact he was in charge now. And in the weeks that followed he'd improved the running of the place, and was bringing in more business.

It was late and Summer was riding the bus back from a gig at the Harrah Casino New Orleans, which was in Poydras Street. She felt it had gone well there, as it was a very posh place with a hotel and club bar on the premises and was very big and colourful. She smiled to herself as she couldn't believe it now, as he'd heard her sing in a down town club. And tonight she'd come up in the world. As the owner had given her a chance to sing tonight, and if she went down well he'd give her three permanent slots with guaranteed good money, and he had done just that.

She couldn't wait to phone Jason in the morning to tell him her news, as she was tired now and was looking forward to her bed, only a short walk after the bus to her place. She was lucky as she managed just to get it, and it was full of students going back to there digs and dorms near their University near the park, so the bus was noisy. So was glade when her stop came in site, only it was also theirs as they pushed pass her to get off first, laughing and shouting among them selves. One thing she hated about New Orleans was that the law on drinking was lax on the age to

start. Mind you it was lax on most rules she felt as she waited for the last one to get off so she could.
The driver then spoke to her, it is all ways like this the last week of August. Trying to cram in as much as they can of pleasure before collage starts in September after spending the summer at their family's home. Summer nodded and got off and started the 10 minute walk to her place.

It was a little cooler after the shower that evening as she slowly walked home. She'd not noticed the gang of youths hanging about on the corner in the shadows till she got near. She was still carrying her knife as she put her fingers around the handle and held it tight. Not that it would be any good with all them she felt. Maybe they will leave her alone as there is so many of them.

She crossed the street just to be sure, she then quicken her pace as they called out to her, pretty girl come play the night is still young. Don't be like that girl we don't mean you any harm
She started running. Only she'd not noticed that the car they were hanging around near belonged to one of them, and he took off in it after her and cut her off.

Summer looked around to see if there was any one about to help her, but no.

By now the others had joined them and before she could draw a breath she was bundled into the boot of the car.

In the dark she felt the car move and knew they were taking her some where isolated. She felt no fear what was the point. Maybe if she was lucky she'd only be violated by a couple of them. She knew one thing she'd make sure she saw their faces so she could remember them all and make them pay.

After a short drive the car stopped and the boot was opened. And the 6 youths were staring at her. Most were drunk and pretend to shag them selves to show they were men. The tallest black bald headed youth had a tattoo on his head of a black Eagle graded hold of her and pulled her out, he was as tall as herself as he pulled her by the arm over to a dilapidated building on the derelict site. Pushed her inside it followed by the other 5. Then told her to strip as the others cheered him on.

Only she now stood her ground, her demeanour had changed. You want me to strip then come do it I dare you, still holding on to the knife in her pocket.

The big black youth all in black leathers turned and spoke to a tubby white youth who didn't seem to be drunk like the others she thought.

He backed away from them and said no way man.

The black guy replied what the fucks wrong with you man go and strip her. Are you a coward or what?

Nothing happened as no one moved, so the big black guy stepped in front of her so they were face to face, "In any other circumstances she'd fancy him as he was beautiful" as he reached out to grab hold of her black cotton top. Summer quickly bought out the knife and slashed him right across his cheek. To the dismay of the other guys blood started to gush out straight into Summers face.

She quickly stepped sideways from him and wiped her face on her sleeve as she held out the flick knife in the others direction.

They were stunned by what had happened, as it was usually easy to have their way with a girl, even two together. This was different.

The big guy shouted out to them while holding a rag against his cheek from the boot of the car. It seemed she had cut him from his jaw line to his ear and it was deep she noticed. He couldn't deal with her as he couldn't let go of the soaked rag. Fuck you lot do something before I bleed to death. Grab her and beat her up before stripping her and gang raping her in stead of standing there like cowards. God she's only a girl? What you fucking well waiting for guys an invitation.

One youth a black thin long haired guy replied, I think you need to go to the Hospital before all your blood is on the ground, which by now they all noticed was soaked in blood. The others went back out and got in the car, the driver turned on the engine ready to leave as they now wanted know part of this. The big guy still stood holding his face. You're a bloody lucky bitch. Just you wait I'll get my own back. I'll find you, you see if I don't and cut you up bad you fucking bitch, turned and walked back out to the car and got in as it was about to drive off without him.

Summer bent and wiped the blood off the knife on the pile of rags next to her, which she believe they were going to gang rape her on. Closed the knife and calmly put it back in her trouser pocket picked up her bag off the ground and walked out into the night and started the short walk out of that area which she didn't know in to her own.

She searched for her smart phone in her bag. One of the gang had taken her bag and throw it into the boot before her, which meant that she lay on top of it making it impossible to get at it, so she could phone 911 the police for help. But know mind she'd managed on her own and come out of it, as she searched for the street name so she could phone a taxi. There was no way she was going to walk the rest of the way home so phoned one.

As for that guy let him try and get me, I'll give him a matching cut on the other side his face. As she heard the taxi man on the phone say he would be 15 minutes, so she sat on the wall out side a house to wait, taking out a mint and popped it into her mouth. She could do with some water but that would have to wait till she got home. Sure in the knowledge that nothing else would happen to her while she waited.

CHAPTER 5

It had been 2 months since Madams accident and Summer's attack. It was November and New Orleans was gearing up for all saints day, then Fringe Festival but first the PO-Boy Festival then Christmas so it was anything but quiet.

Summer had not even remembered the attack on her by the gang, Same with all the other unpleasant incidence in her life. As she behaved as if they hadn't even happen, or had happened to someone else.

Summer sat in the Balcony club bar, it was lunch time and she'd been spending a lot of time there during the day. Helping Jason out as he was still a little nerves at being in charge. You wouldn't believe that he was 4 years older than her and would soon be 21. As she watched him dither over how he should pay the tradesmen.

The grocery delivery man wanted payment there and then, Jason wanted to pay monthly. He knew his mother paid weekly, but he was not his mother. In the end Summer had to step in as she knew he'd paid him weekly up till now but he was not happy with the arrangement.

Jason what does it matter how you pay people if it works why change it just because it was your mothers way she told him?

Jason gave in to her words, how is it you're so wise for such a young one. And walked off to get cash and pay the tradesman, putting the bill in the accounts drawer. It was harder than he realised running three business in one. Glade that it was the quieter season till Christmas week and new year eve. He'd not tell her how he felt as she seemed always in control of her life speaking softly to him self. " He'd not even noticed the cat wasn't around any more as he'd been so busy" Walked back in to the bar reluctantly, having to give in.

Summer's gig's thinned out in the four club's she played at to one a week at each one where she always had two. But the Casino was still regular and the CO Mr Sheldon Ruffin had got her gigs at the country Club at weekends once a month also at a night club in Baton Rouge the capital.

He'd collared her after the second gig at his place, and said he thought she could go far with her talent, and with his connections he'd make sure she did. "He was a very tall tubby man in his 50's of Irish American decent, and when he came in to the Casino all could feel his presence and stop what they were doing as he passed." She felt he could make her life difficult in New Orleans if she didn't comply with his wish's.

A voice in her head said you can't kill him if he did just that, like the others. Summer shook her head to dismiss the voice from her head, as she'd only hurt her Stepfather. All the same she agreed only if they had it down in writing, an agreement between them. Which he agreed to, as he liked the idea, and felt she had a good business head on her young shoulders.

Mr Ruffin had never had a woman singer before to manage. He'd got 2 men on his books and they made him money, not that he needed the money as his Casino brought in a good income, as did his other business. He'd decided to sit Summer down in his office a week later to sign the contract after she'd read it.

The voice in her head had only started being there recently told her not to sign, she tried to ignore it and read the contract which seemed fair so signed.

You won't regret it Summer, I'll make you a star you see. Don't get me wrong girl I'm doing this because I believe you will go far. Also I suppose you could say it is my hobby away from my business world. The contract I believe covers every thing, costumes and transport. And I have a man who will be your body guard and eye's and ear's when you're gigging out of Town, so no worries on your part.

She replied that the contract was okay. But I don't need a body guard?

Call me Sheldon and you will you see. He'll also get you to your gigs take care of luggage and the transport which will be a small RV, I have a couple of them. One is already being used by my two male singers on the road. My other one you will use. You're need a woman with you to take care of clothes and make up while on the road. I'll get my PR to range that. So miss, as he poured out two whisky in crystal glass's here's to you and your musical career.

To the new year and a new start in 2023. For now you can relax and leave every thing in my PR's hands. Your first gig hopefully will in February in Baton Rouge under the new contract, so not that far away. My PR will contact you here when you are to sing and where With that he picked up a large fat cigar cut the end off in an ash tray and lite it then turned picked up his black Stetson which had a gold band around it and a gold chip at the front. He put it on, and it made him look even taller than his 6ft 4inch's tall and left. He was the first person she'd met taller than herself.

Leaving her in disbelief by it all, as it all had happened so quickly. After all it was still only November and she'd only been in New Orlean a little over seven month's not years. Checked her watch it was lunch time, she'd been there well over an hour just to read and sign the contract, picking up her copy. She'd go show it to Jason after she'd picked up lunch and some groceries then home to her place to feed Maggie, who now lived in doors and the area around the house. Not venturing out of the front gate. She'd got used to Maggie and couldn't imagine not having her, as she waited for the Streetcar to take her down Canal Street the hub of the city with it's 4 lane road with Palm tree's lining the middle of it, a smaller version of Paris's Avenue des Champs Elysees that lead to the Eiffel tower. Someday she'd go there.

Now to get off at the end of Canal and walk straight in to Royal Street, where she'd get groceries, her head still full of her new singing career. Maybe one day we'll sing in Paris her voice replied. Go away shaking her head as she walked towards the 24 hour grocer's. What's happing to me grabbing hold of her head and shouted go away "right there in Royal with people looking at her strangely".

People are looking at us the voice in her head said. This is not real I'm not going mad under her breath as she hurried on in to the shop and disappeared inside. Took a deep breath and told herself she was just over tired and imaging it with all that had happened. "The voice in her head realised she'd better call it for a while in her head until she was needed".

Back home now and feeling more at ease with her self, she realised she was just tired what with helping out Jason with his accounts and paperwork, then the gigs late in to the night she'd have to try and take things a little slower. Then realised she couldn't not with her new gigs, she'd have to spend less time helping Jason.

December came and Christmas week came around and the City was even more festive than usual, even the big oaks that were lined up to the main gates to Albany park were lite up with fairy lights. Summer was really happy to be there, as this would be her first without her parents. So this year she'd not be assaulted by her stepfather after his Christmas town hall Ball, then the new year one. She remembered that her mother always ran the sitter home as he was always worse for wear so he told her mother. It was so he could get her alone to rape. Girl she told her self stop thinking about them and get on enjoy the season of good will.

Even the Casino was putting on a big do at the town hall with the Mayor and dignitaries going, herself singing with the band she'd been using for a couple of her gigs for a while. Even Sheldon had signed them up to back her on her tour, which pleased her as it meant she had people around she knew. Maggie rubbed herself around her bringing her back to the job at hand decorating the tiny tree she'd bought at the market and also the decoration's she'd also brought from there. I'll feed you when I'v finished here. And no knocking it off the low small table, which was a find in a skip while jogging. You'd be surprised what you find in a skip Maggie. She just meowed loudly as she was hungry. Okay old girl I'll get us some food quickly putting the star on top of the 3 foot real tree with it's roots still in tacked she was going to plant it in the backyard afterwards. And went and got food. Sorry girl I have a full week of gigs, so you're on your own I'll leave the radio on for you and food.

Summer got ready for her first gig on a Monday as it was Christmas. She didn't mind as money for that week's gigs was doubled. And the two major ones with Sheldon's Ball then the Mayor's ball, she was going to get 2 large payments, same for her backing band.

Looking though her improved wardrobe of clothes and two evening dress's for the Ball's, which she'd bought second hand at Swap Rags Vintage and Vice and Graft Vintage shop's in the French Quarter. Which meant she had managed to save money, so to night she was going to wear a pair of red leather trousers and an abstract printed blouse with her black leather high heeled boots which her mother bought her 2 years earlier for Christmas. They were too good to bin and were comfortable with 2 inch heels making her over 6 foot which she liked. She'd decided to wear something different each night but keep the boots on. Now looking in the mirror she felt she looked good with her light make up and her long hair up in a roll. She heard the taxi buzz her to say he was there. No way this festive time was she walking to and from any gig's. Not till warmer weather gathering up her shoulder bag kissed a well fed Maggie who was now asleep on her bed, turned on the radio in the kitchen and double locket the back door then the front door and walked out to the waiting taxi feeling good in herself, she'd had no more voices in her head and tonight she was going to enjoy herself.

Christmas week seemed to fly by, but was great fun on her part. Christmas dinner was held in Jason's restaurant in the lunch hour on Christmas Day. The night before had been Christmas Eve and Jason layed on a buffet and party for the staff and she attend, it was the first time there was a staff party as Madam was too mean to spend money. And to the staffs surprise there was a pay rise in the wage packet. Jason had hired an accountant and business assistant so she could get on with her own life. Now every one was looking forward to new year's. And Jason was laying on a big party for friends staff and customers. He'd hoped Summer and the band would appear, but she had to tell him she was playing at the Maison de La Luz Hotel, in there conference room, the Mayor yearly Ball she told Jason.

She was sorry as she so wanted to go, but a job is a job and she was under contract to do all the gigs that Sheldon had layed on for her. His Ball had been a great success so he told her on the phone the next morning "Some of his big business friend's we're there from other states, and stayed over at Sheldon's Casino Hotel for that night." And they told Sheldon that they could get Summer more gigs from club owners they knew, as they were impressed by her singing. Sheldon then relayed that to her. Club owners in there State's would love to hire her to sing on a regular basic. So he gave them the go a head, and they were to deal with his PA who would organise it on her behave.

For once she was not too happy with all the new gigs without first asking her, as she had a life beside singing. As it didn't give her time to live. And what about Maggie she told him? She couldn't just up and leave her in the house for so long, she'd starve she told him on the phone that morning.

He'd told her to buy a harness and take the cat with her. As for the new gigs, it would give her the opportunity to play all over the country and might even put her name in lights.

He told her that he could see himself as another Colonel Parker Elvis Presleys manager. And like him, you are under contract then rang off. Leaving her stunned, it seemed she was trapped by that contract. She tried to remember if it said she would have to do all gigs under contract. And got her copy and read the small print, and it did say that. So there was know way out but go along with the gigs. At least she'd could bring Maggie.

She'd put what Sheldon had said out of her mind until tomorrow. Jason had asking her to come to his New Year party and sing couple of song's as well to get the party going. There would be many times when the gigs Sheldon got her clashed with things she wanted to do like this time at Jason's. And there was know way she could get out of it. God she wished she'd never got mixed up with him. It was her own thought as she'd under estimated how many gigs he would be able to get her.

Summer sat there on the stage in the conference room, which was set up as a ballroom, while the boys set up their instruments on stage. Piped music played loudly from speakers on the high ceiling, as people came in all dressed in evening wear, long evening dresses and the men wore dress suit's. Summer and the band were dressed the same. Then the piped music stopped and a man came on stage from behind curtains hung at a side door and asked it they were ready.

Summer replied yes. So he introduced them to the room of people, then he joined the people in the room, as the band started to play, then she sang along.

After an hour she'd noticed know one was listen to them, they could be any band singing anything. The New Orleans business men and the rich couples were more interested in talking shop and drinking expensive wine. Each woman trying to out do the other by all their fine jewellery.

By the end of the even with only half hour break, it seemed to her a wasted evening on her's and the bands part. She could have been enjoying herself at Jason's. And she was sure the band would rather have spent time with their family's. Even the money didn't make up for a lousy evening.

Summer waited while the band packed up. They two felt as she did and told her so. But once again they were under contract. It was now gone midnight night and 2023 they all should be looking to a happy and good new year.

They all said they had been happier just playing in New Orleans clubs before they departed company till the next gig in a weeks time.

They all got into their van. While she climb into her taxi. She wondered if she'd drop in at Jasons before bed looking at her watch. It was 12 57 am, by the time she got there the festive would be over so changed her mind and just let the taxi take her home.

Next morning came around as Maggie licked her face to wake her. Summer mounded at her as she had a headache and turned over away from Maggie. Maggie was not going to give up as she was hungry. So in the end she gave up and sat up in bed and stroked Maggie as she looked at the clock, it was nearly 11 am so not bad. Okay girl I'll get your tuna. Got up went to the loo to pee then into the kitchen and got some food for herself as well, a muffin and coffee and went and sat on the couch switching on the TV to hear the local and national new. After 20 minutes of uninteresting news, she got herself another muffin and coffee and sat with her feet up on the coach trying not to move the now happy Maggie curled up on the end.

Summer was about to phone Jason while she layed there eating, when a news story shocked her. The news reader said that Sheldon Ruffin was found dead in his suite at his Casino Hotel this morning by a cleaner. We don't know yet how he died. He was a big name in New Orleans government and business world and will be missed. The news reader also said that the Casino brought a lot of business to New Orleans, Who will take it over is unknown, as it is believed he had no family. He will be missed as he was a larger than life man. We will keep you in touch as we get more news. This is WGNO NEWS signing off for now.

Summer sat in shock, as she couldn't believe it. She'd seen him at the Mayors Ball last night surrounded by young pretty girls as always. He looked in good health. He even reminded her during the interval that they had to start rehearsal next week, ready for the tour, as it had been moved up to 2nd week in January with the new gigs. Just then her mobile phone rang, it was Bryan.

Have you heard about Sheldon , he's dead?

Where does that leave us with the tour Summer?

No idea sorry, we will have to just wait and see if someone contacts us from his office.

I know it sounds terrible but in a way I feel relieved that the prospect that we might not have to go on tour, I know you wern't please with how many gigs he'd got for us. Without any regard for our welfare. What do you say Summer?

I still can't believe he's gone Bryan. All we can do is wait. We'll still rehears the new pieces just for us and the local Clubs till we know. Don't worry see you as usual rest now bye ringing off.

Maggie I'm going to Jasons shouldn't be long, talking to a sleeping cat.

Every one she knew was talking about Sheldon, Maybe because he over shadowed every one with his presence being such a big tall man, and that bloody hat and cigar, which she hated as he'd puff it into your face while still talking to you. Very rude she felt.

Jason gave her a big hug as she walked though the door of his bar. Knew you'd come this morning. You won't be touring this new year now thank god. It means your'e be around to play here as usual and to keep me company, letting her go so she could breath.

Jason I don't know anything yet, as it is too soon. He only passed away last night.

What do you think he died of? It won't be from a heart attack as he didn't have one. And all he could see when he looked at people was dollar signs and how he could capitalise on you.

Thats not very nice Jason, and in any case you didn't know him. You never met him did you? When father died he came around to see if the place was worth buying. Mama was up for it, but the solicitor said as the place was mine it was up to me. I might have been young but know way was I selling pops place, which he worked hard to make it what it is today not Mama. So that's how I know.

I'm sorry Jason you never said. Even Bryan phoned me pleased Sheldon was dead. I didn't wish him that Jason, just for him to see us as people not dollar signs as you said. Wonder how he died?

Maybe someone murdered him, he must have made enemies over the years don't you think?

Guess so Jason, we'll just have to wait and see.

Two weeks passed, and Sheldon had a big funeral before his coffin was transferred to Dallas to be buried. It turned out that was where he came from and still had a very old rich mother living there.

Summer and Bryan had heard nothing about the tour. Summer wasn't going to contact Sheldon's PA to find out.

While rehearing with the band in the hall of the local church, two policemen came in and interrupted them while playing. They were there to find out about the night of the 31 of December. When did we last see and speak to Mr Ruffin? To Summers surprise they asked if they got on with him. Did we like him?

Summer couldn't believe it, why ask us as we only worked for him that was all. We never mixed or had dealings in Ruffin business or personal life.

Summer asked why are you asking us Mr policeman? I mean we only saw him when we played at his Casino, and the Mayor's Ball sir.

Bryan suddenly blurted out, was he murdered is that why you're questioning us?

It is a suspicious death. We are following up on leads, and people he had dealings with like yourselves. We'll I think that will be all for now, and with that they left. Leaving them all stunned that they could be thought of as murders.

They evidently don't have any leads, that's why they came here. The police here are good at hassling young people but not solving a real crime Paul replied. I wouldn't worry they won't be back you see.

Summer couldn't believe he was murdered. I mean he was a powerful man with body guards as well, and they had guns, saw the bulge in the jacket's. Even if he had enemy's, his place was like Fort Knox.

How do you know all that replied Shawn the smallest of the band members asked her, and what's Fort Knox?

It's a military Federal Gold depository reservation in North Kentucky, it's a federal god depository, where they save money in case it's needed I think? Thought every one knew that. Something I learned at school. As for the rest you asked about I just do.

Now what do we do guy's ? Do we keep on rehearing now or leave it for the day, as I don't feel like practicing right now Paul asked them?

Let's call it a day for now meet up in 3 days here to go over our songs again, she hoped thing might look better then. Maybe we'll even know where we stand with the Tours, what do you guys say?

They all agreed with her and left there gear in a room off the church hall. Bryan double locked it as that area was known for it's house robbery's even though it was a poor area.

Two more weeks pass and they had heard nothing about their contract, altho there was new management at the Casino, now they were well in to February.

While she was at Jason's restaurant having lunch with him, an elderly man came up to their table and introduced himself as The Mayor's PA, hope i'm not interrupting your meal.

I'm here on behave of the Mayor to ask if you and your band would play at the Mardi Gras ball at Hotel Monteleone on 214 Royal Street in the French Quarter. You may know it because of it's Carousel rotating Piano Bar and lounge. But it also has a large Ballroom as well. The Ball is on the last evening of Mardi Gras. What do you say?

I'd love to and I'm sure the guys will say the same thank you.

Good I will forward you the time of the Ball and of course your fee is to be the same as the last ball you played at, if that's okay with you? If you give me your email address. I'll leave you to finish your meal in peace, it looks good.

Summer couldn't believe that she'd still get gigs from the Mayor even without Sheldon. So Jason the contract is know longer, as the ball was on Sheldon's list for us. The new PA would have emailed us to let us know, and the fee would have been fixed by the new management as they take 25 percent. I must phone Bryan and let him know the good news. Kissing Jason on the lips, as she was a happy person as it meant they were free to get their own gigs again.

Jason was taken aback by the kiss and just stared at her, as he had so wanted to do that to her. He'd had hidden feelings for her for so long. Maybe there is hope as he watched her talk on the phone to Bryan.

After she'd finished talking on the phone. Turn to Jason, it's funny that when people start being nasty to me or you like your mother. Something happened to make things right. The Gods are good to us, what do you say?

It had never crossed his mind till now, and said just that to her, lets put it out of our minds and enjoy our meal.

The week of Mardi Gras came around, and it was her first one, and Jason was going to take her where she could get a good view of the floats. As each area had their own day, with the French quarter last and the best. Beaded neckless were every where hanging on trees and fences, walls even cars. Summer wondered who cleared the hundreds of them up from each area, then what happened to them? She asked a tall thick set uniformed policeman, but he didn't know. No one she asked seemed to know.

Why worry your head about it Summer, as it's not important now is it?

Jason words Made her mad, as she said of course it's important as it could mean they go in land fill. Which is not good for the land don't you think?

Y'es of course I do, but there is nothing we can do about it.

Summer gave up talking to him about it. Now she'd seen it, she'd talk to the Mayor at the Ball tonight and find out where they went. If it was Landfill or a tip then shed campaign to get them recycled for next year. No point in telling Jason all this she felt.

The floats and parade thou the French quarter was much more unruly than the other areas floats, with young drunk girls showing their bare tits to the passing floats and parades, young men baring their bums. Everywhere there was litter. And people drinking in the streets and being sick, then just dropping their take away, mugs and getting a new drink in a new one instead of refilling them. The weather was warming up in March so the air smell of booze sick and spices, also sweat with all those crowds. Summer told Jason she'd give it a miss next year.

I love it babe, and it brings in a lot of money that normally this time of year wouldn't see. In any case it's been going since forever girl. You're get used to the smell and noise after a while.

She didn't agree, but just nodded okay. Looked at her watch she had to go get change for the gig at 9. Luckily she had been given a room at Hotel Monteleone free of charge to change in and the band. They had all left there clothes for tonight there that morning. Jason had given her a beautiful mask to wear and a red and gold feathered hair clip as it was a period custom ball. Summer hired herself a red gown with gold and black touches around the edges and 2 inch gold high heels from the custom hire shop in the French Quarter. She'd not had time to try it on yet so hoped it fitted. The band were going to wear ruffled shirts and knee length trouser and long socks with buckled black painting shoes which they hated. And couldn't see why they couldn't wear a tuxedo in stead.

Summer reminded them they were being paid well, and it was only for a few hours.And they was not reason to be embarrassed as they knew know one there at that rich man's Ball.

The night went well, and they played mostly RB music and finished with Jazz. In the interview she tried to talk to the Mayor but he was busy talking to a group of friends. Even afterwards at 1am she tried but know joy his body guards wouldn't let her near him as he left to go home. So she still had know idea about the horrid beads.

So said her goodbyes to the guys in the band. Guys I'll phone you about our next gig, and she left to phone a cab outside. After along wait a voice on the line told her she'd have a long wait as all his cabs were booked for the next hour or so. He reminded her it is Mardi Gras miss. After his words she decided to walk after all it was only about 40 minutes walk if she took the short cut. And the fresh air would do her good.

There was a light chilly breeze as she walked to the corner of Royal and across at St Anns in to the east of Royal then up the rest of Esplanade Avenue, There were a lot of people about with the same idea as herself. So she felt safe walking up to Rampart Street and across it in to Lous Armstrong Park, and walked through it heading towards North Robertson Street just a step from the park and she'd be home. She could see the lights of her street as she walked through the park.

She had a bad headache starting and couldn't wait to get home when a hand went over her mouth and she was lifted off her feet and carried to the end of the park to a waiting van as she kicked and squirmed in his firm hold.

Told you baby I'd get my revenge after your knife attack on my face. Now it's your turn as he got to the van. Summer could see one person at the wheel as he let go of her with one hand and tried to bundle her into the open door of the van.

Summer had know idea who he was and what he was talking about as she'd not used her knife on any one. He must have made a mistake.
Who ever you are I don't know what you're talking about?
Oh it's you all right, and when I saw your name on the poster for the Mardi Gras Ball I saw my chance and waited outside the Hotel till you came out and bided my time till now, as he tried to heaved her into the van as he let go of his grip on her as he did so.

Suddenly her mind became blank and she passed out. Then she landed just inside the door of the van on her bottom, her leg's hanging out in the door way, mad as hell she kicked out at the figure in front of her as she remembered promising herself she'd cut the other side of his face if he did come back. How dare he think he can hurt her as her face screw up in angry as she kicked out at him again before he could retaliate.

Got out the van and as her feet touched the road she leaped at him her nails out she clawed at his face and eyes, as he tried franticly to pull this mad girl off him. He knew once again he'd been wrong to underestimated her.

The driver hearing the commotion got out and came around to the back, only to see his mate on the ground with a mad girl clawing and biting his face while on top of him. The noise she was making gave him the chives as he tried to pull her of his mate. But know joy as she turned blood dripping from her mouth and hissed at him and went back to biting black guy.

The driver looked at his mate, as she lifted her head again for a second and he saw that his mate had a gouge in his neck so took off like a bat out of hell in his van out of the park and kept going till he got to his place. He couldn't believe what he'd just saw, as he tried to pour himself a drink his hand was shacking as he did so, and sat on a chair, his Pit bull came out of the bedroom and up to him putting his head on his lap as if to reasure him he was safe now. One thing he knew he was going to keep what had just happened tonight to himself as he believed she was a real witch or zombie as he cuddled his dog tightly to him.

Summer finished biting him and was satisfied he was dead. Got up and walked calmly to the park fountain and took out her hankie from her bag and soaked it. Then calmly washed the blood off her face and hands. Put it back in the water and soaked it then went back to the van and wiped her finger prints off the places she knew she'd touched. Then went back again soaked the dress she'd warn at the Ball in the water and went back again soaking his jacket and face as he lay there dead. Funny she didn't even know his name as she looked at his torn apart flesh on his face and neck, Man you shouldn't have tried again as I'm her protecting Angel. God I hope I have cleaned you enough, then remember that forensic can get DNA from the bites.

Looked around to see if anyone was about and saw she was alone so lifted him up and put him on the front seat of the van. checking for a lighter or matches in his pockets and found a lighter and a tin of wacky baccy, she knew just what to do as she picked up the half empty whisky bottle in the van and stuffed a rag in the top lite it and collected her clothes and throw the bottle in through the open window. stood back away from it as she put the wet dress back in her overnight bag, with the hankie, making sure there was no visible blood on it or her. As she waited for the van to catch fire.

She knew it wouldn't take long as the van was full of rubbish. And she was right turned and walked towards home.

She hoped the street had been empty all that time, as she'd not heard footsteps or a car pass. Then her house came into view. She walking up the steps to the veranda and throw the front door, and as she walked into her house she was now unaware of what she had just done. Her head now was full of the Mardi Gras beads, tomorrow she'd go on line to see if she could find out. Maggie came out of the bedroom meow and rub herself around her.

Don't know about you old girl but I am hungry how about a snack before bed, how about you? It had been was a good night, the people listened a lot of the time walking in to the kitchen to make a sandwich and get Maggie a dish of food followed by Maggie.

CHAPTER 6

Louie Armstrong park was cordon off with police tape. Not a good start to the beginning of the festive season the French district police chief said as he stood looking at the disfigured burned face of the dead body in the burned out car. All around were remnants of Mardi Gras. The City wasn't even awake yet as he looked at his watch, it was only 5am. And by rights he should still be in his bed if it wern't for the fact the guy was murdered.

Never before had they come across it, only animals bite lumps out of the flesh. Even bringing burned you could see the bites. So we have an animal on the loose in New Orleans that was dangerous talking to his sergeant who then relayed it to the men standing around in a daze. Surly an animal couldn't start a fire Sergeant?

Until we know what king of animal we can't do anything until the autopsy is done. So make it a priority? And check what was in that tin on the seat next to him with the lighter near bye.

CSI Morgan replied, sir there are no pieces of flesh found around the body or on it.
Everyone stood silent as know one could fathom what could possibly done such a thing.

Summer awoke to Maggie right in her face licking her. Smiled and lifted herself up her head turned and looked at the clock it was gone 12. She'd never slept so long. But at least her headache had gone stretching and sat up. I smell Maggie, a good soak in the bath before breakfast.
Maggie meowed at that as she was hungry. Okay I'll feed you first and make coffee to drink while in the bath. Walked in to the kitchen and turned on the Radio to a music channel, she wasn't in the mood for the news just in case something bad had happened as this was New Orleans after all.

In the bathroom she took off her pyjamas and looked at her self in the mirror.To her surprise she had bruises on her arms, and her neck was sore as she tried to look at the back of it. Only to see what looked like finger marks as she held her hand mirror up to see it, as she lifted her hair up. Summer dropped the mirror and took a step back, how the fuck could I get these she said out loud. There is know way as I came straight home without any bother as usual. Am I going mad. Turned and got in the hot bubble bath to think, how could this be happen going over the evening and the walk after to her place. Know nothing happened. Maybe I had a nightmare and did this to my self in my sleep, that can be the only logical answer she could think of, which made her feel a little better as she drank her coffee.

After soaking for a while she'd put the bruises out of her mind and started thinking about Mardi Gras. How each districts of the Mardi Gras parade's we're different crowd wise. Still lots of beads but no rude drunk girls and boys, more of a family affair with local business and the hospital float. Much nicer than the French District parade. And those beads sitting with a bowl of cereal in front of the Laptop she went on line to find out just where the beads go?

Summer couldn't believe what she was reading. The beads were shipped from China by the ton. Also each year an estimated 25 million pounds of plastic beads are dumped on the City after Mardi Gras.
Orleans Sanitation workers were dispatched one year to clean out the clogged catch basins. In which they found more than 46 tons "93 pounds" of beads.

A Dr Howard Mielke of Pharmacology specifically worried about the amount of lead these beads distribute in to the street. He discovered that the majority of high levels were in the soil found along parade routes. Summer kept reading, and found that in 2014 the City was forced to spend nearly 1-5 million dollars on Sanitation after collecting an eye popping 1.758 tons of trash, beads solo cups and styrofoam take away containers all going to land fill, which are already over falling in the United States. She found on line there were organisation's trying to change things by collecting some beads and recycling them also selling them. And found there is a petition to ban them, currently it has 15,000 signatures. Professor Naohiro Kato created biodegradable bead from microscopic algae at the States University.

After reading that she decided to sign the petition to ban them. She also decided to keep what she'd read. And sent the information to both the Major's email address and Jasons email address and the newspapers.

After all that reading she felt like some air, got herself a glass of juice and went and sat on the veranda. Maggie decided to stay inside all though she'd left the front door open while out there for her cat.

Her neighbour's we're already out there as the weather was not to bad for March. Mrs Robinson was sitting eating while Mr Robinson was reading the newspaper while eating lunch. On seeing Summer Mrs Robinson called out hallo then asked her if she enjoyed her first Mardi Gras, as they them selves don't go any more. Once you'v seen it that's enough?

Summer told her not really, she enjoyed the floats not the crowds in the French quarter, too many drunks and rude young people there. I'll give it a miss next year myself. She hoped Mrs Robertson wouldn't go on talking as she just wanted to relax, but for nearly an hour she chatted on. While Summer tried her best not to seem rude and just muted in reply most of the time till she'd had enough and decided to go get dressed and visit Jason.

Frenchman Street had no floats in their area so no beads or trash. It was nice to see the flower pots outside his bar and restaurant without a bead in sight. She knew that the guest house part of the business was full with young people staying for Mardi Gras week. She could hear a band playing from a distance away and hoped that it wasn't what she believed she was hearing which sounded like heavy metal which she disliked.

Walked up the steps in to the bar which she had already thought was full of young people. And realised it was heavy metal and decided to give it a miss and turned to walk back out before she was seen, only to be seen by Jason who was pleased to see her.

Hi baby hoped you'd come, kissing her on the cheek. How was it last night? Trying to be heard over the noisy band.

It was a great night they loved us, and the money as you know was good. So all round a great night talking loudly above the noise. Do you mind if I don't stay as I had a headache last night after playing and it hasn't really gone. And what with this music?
You'v come all this way stay, I'll get one of the girls to get you a couple of pills, what do you say giving her one of his puppy dog looks?

No pills just in case it is not headache pills, as I know some here take ecstasy and smoke marijuana.

Baby really? How do you know that?
I stayed here remember, and I sing here so of course I know so do you Jason. Not that I care so long as I don't take any. I'm sorry Jason but with the noise from the band I'll give it a miss. Let me know when the heavy metal band is not playing

then I'll visit? With that she walked back out the door which was only a couple of feet away. Leaving Jason disappointed as he so wanted to spend more time with her after that kiss.

The air along the River walk with its palm trees and bench's we're a relief from the smell of and noise of Jasons bar as she sat out side the Aquarium of the Americas beside the River. There was still trash and beads around but the peace and air was refreshing. In the distance moored up was a big white paddle steamer waiting for it's passengers. Without hesitation She got up and walked along towards it till she got to the kiosk and got herself a ticket to travel on it up the river and back. She needed a change and a river trip might put her in a better mood. Her neck was still sore and her head ache had started to come back, also she didn't feel herself for some reason.

The ship was only half full as she sat on deck and watched the boats go up and down. She knew the Mississippi went nearly all the way to where her family live in Seattle, now why did she think about her parents again as she'd not for a good while and quickly put them out of her mind.

She wished she'd bought a flask of coffee with her as she was getting thirsty rubbed her neck, she could feel indentations in it as if nails had dug in to it. The ride had not helped her mood as she got off, so decided to buy a take away and take it home and go though the new piece of music she written on the old piano she'd bought.
Singing for her own pleasure always lifted her spirits.
After buying a Muffulettas with salami shaved ham mortadella and sliced provolone cheese salty olive oil and pickled vegetables in a large round sesame crusty loaf, which would do her for two meals and a coffee to drink on the way home. The smell of the

loaf made her even more hungry as she bit into it as she walked towards her place.

After eating most of the loaf she went through her new music while singing, and had started to feel better. Went and sat outside only to be confronted by the locals who had heard her sing and cheered her as she came out and stood on the veranda.

One local had his Guitar and asked her to sing along with him accompanying her. How could she say no, and sang a song the locals would know, and by the early evening a party had started up in the street, people had bought out chairs from off their verandas and drink some even food and put it on a trestle table that someone had set up in the street.

For the first time she felt at ease around them and gave it her all singing her headache now gone, The evenings festive went on in to the night as the locals sang and talked and enjoyed them selves with her. Around 2 she could hardly keep her eyes open and had to call it a day, and went in and fell asleep on top of the bed fully clothes content.

Two weeks later the police were know where nearer finding out who or what killed the guy in the park. And they'd managed to keep how he died out of the press. Only the driver who was there at the scene of the murder knew it was a mad girl. And he had no intention of telling any one all though he had nightmares most nights.

Mardi Gras had been late this year because of really bad weather in February. Now it would soon be St Patrick's Day in March, and Summer and the band were playing at Tracey's bar in the Irish Channel spot bar in Magazine Street.

Molly's at the market is where the Irish parade start's and end at the bar with an Irish party with herself and the band playing. A gig she got herself. And it went well giving them a permanent nights work every 2 weeks.

Their calendar of gigs for the spring and summer was full. Summer also got them a spot at the Congo Square New World Rhythms Festival. With expert drumming dancing and crafts also delicious free food in the square. Thankfully it was nothing like the Mardi Gras crowd. It was more for family's and she really enjoyed playing with the band for free.

Now it was April and the festival season continued on with Gay Easter Parade. People dressed up in their frilliest Sunday best then marched or rode in carriages past the gays bars in the french quarter. Summer watched it all from Jackson Square with Jason and a lot of other tourist gathering on the pavements around the square. She'd never seen anything like it and enjoyed it.

Then the French Quarter Festival in mid April with stages and bands playing funk, jazz and latin Rhythms and Cajun brass bands and R an B, plus free food stalls operated by the City's most popular restaurants. Summer and the band paid for a spot so they could put a stage up at it. A gain no money but she told the boys it would be good publicity for them. And she was right they went down well and got some more gigs from it.

The last week of April they had another important gig like the last one in the French Quarter, only this time they'ed be playing with lots of other bands all around them all playing at the same time in the Fair Grounds Race Course, with stalls selling wares and food and the different bands playing.Then the last night a famous name band would finish off the festival.

After watching Willie Nelson who looked good for being so old. Someone near her told her they had been coming to it for years, and heard the who band there several years back, and the late

David Bowie and even Elvis Costello. He told her he had heard her play and enjoyed it. Summer thanked him, and said she had to leave to get a bus as it was so late and hundreds would have the same idea. And she was right, as hundreds all rushed out of the gates to get the bus. Her band had the right idea they had left hours earlier.

The same elderly man told her she had a hope in hell of getting a bus or taxi with all the crowds. He'd got his scooter in the local pub near by carpark, and would drop her at the end of Canal, what do you say. You might get a bus to where ever you're staying along there?

Thanks but I'll walk as I live near here. And New Orleans is not that big is it.

Suit yourself as he stormed off leaving her trying not to get crushed by the crowds as she tried getting throw the gates in one piece. Only to see a full bus go by. And a long queue at the bus stop also not a taxi in sight. Oh we'll girl you're going to have to walk like many of them here.

Checked her Map on her phone and found if she walked along Gentilly Blvd along by the race course, at the end was Esplanade Avenue and walk down it towards the river she'd come to the side of Louis Armstrong park and along side the park was Robertson Street, so not as far as she thought as she set off.

As she turned in to Esplanade the elderly gently man rode by on his scooter. Pulled up a little in front of her and got off and stood beside it as if waiting for her. Now what the hell did he want she thought? Walking towards him she'd ignore him and if he starts to speak she'd not answer as all she wanted was to get home as she was tired.

The elderly man had a reputation among the ladies in Treme where he lived alone, "As a pervert". He said he was a widow of several years only he still needed a woman, any woman too fuck.

He couldn't see why ladies found him repulsive he told her. After all he felt he had a lot to offer. Even if It meant he had to engage in conversation when he saw the opportunity. None of the ladies he assaulted had reported him, so he'd kept on doing it. And now he wanted her as his next victim as he watched her walk towards him. Summer had heard every word but thought he was either drunk or a madman as they were in a street with people about so paid him no he'd

He got the chloroform out of his bag that was on the back of his scooter and the rag and pored the sweet-smelling liquid solvent on it and waited for her.

As summer got near him she thought about crossing the road, no why after all her Street was off the side she was on. Esplanade was a wide road with a wide grass verge with trees running down the middle of it. Suddenly she felt faint and blackout for a second. She was now only a couple of feet away from him.

He was going to take the opportunity seeing her leaning against the steps of a terrace house next to him, to grab her and put the cloth over her face. Then he hoped to drag her to the middle of the road on the verge under the cover of a large bush and Palm tree. As he got next to her and bent down to put his hand on her neck.

She was ready for him as she turned her head around. As he tried to put the cloth over her nose she look up at him with a monstrous look on her face as she lunged up at him taking him by surprise and bit a lump of flesh out of his neck and swallowed then she bit in to his cheek taking a large lump out of it.

The man was now stunned by what had just happened and tried hard to pull himself away as she was now laying over the steps with him on top of her, her hand's holding his head in front of her as she eat his flesh till she felt he was lifeless. Pushed him off her and got up. She was covered in his blood and there was no water about to clean herself or him. All she could do was tear with her knife the area's on his neck and cheek she'd touch so as not to leave evidence. She was dying for a wee so wee over his lifeless body, that should take care of finger prints on his coat she hoped?

She walked down to the bottom of Esplanade to the river, ran along too riverwalk hoping not to see anyone on the way. She got to the only place in that area there was no barrier wall in front of the river and climb over the railings and jumped into the river hoping the water would clean her clothes as well and clean her self. If someone had seen she'd pretend she was drunk. All went well and know one saw her as far as she knew.

She walked down her Street soaking wet, till she got outside her place. Checking to see there was no one about she took off all her clothes and left them there under the veranda then went inside got a black bag and went back out and put her clothes and shoes in to it. Then put the bag back under the house hoping Summer didn't come across it. And went back inside and showered. Maggie all this time was asleep on the bed in the spare room, so she made herself a coffee put on her pyjamas and got into bed and drank it down while thinking this was the first time she'd done a normal thing like her other half and found she liked being on the outside. Then layed down and went to sleep. Only to awake as her normal self, who had know recollection on what had happened last night.

The next morning Mr Maddox got up at 9am dressed got his wallet and was off to buy his morning news paper and sit and read it at his favourite Cafe till he knew the rest of his family had got up and gone to school and work, and the chaos in the house would be over, which usually took over an hour. Then he could safely return home to peace. Opening his front door on Esplanade and stepped out onto his porch and went to walk down the steps. Couldn't believe what his eyes were seeing, as it was beyond his imagination and quickly took a step back.

He was relieved he'd not eaton as he felt sick at the sight of the persons face, and even in the cooler heat of early morning the smell was unbearable, his steps were also covered in blood. He'd left his phone as usual when going to the Cafe in door so went back inside and dialled 111.

After a couple of hours with the body and CSI doing there thing, the police were now interviewing the family. As they couldn't understand how they didn't hear anything.

It's a big house his wife replied and we sleep up stairs the children at the back. I sleep with ear plugs as my husband snores. My husband can sleep though any noise sir so I am sorry we are of know help. When can we use our front steps ?

The Sergeant turned to the husband and told him that he'd need to wash the steps with bleach before they could use it in another hour.

The 2 boys of 8 and 10 wanted to see the blood the older 15 year old girl thought they were sick. And then an argument started between them. Poor Mr Maddox had enough and went out the back in to the yard and climb over the fence to his friends house and then out though his house so he could go to the Cafe and get some peace.

His friend didn't mind and said he'd join him at the Cafe. As he knew how bad it could get between kids of different ages and sex. With his own two who were University age kids so he understood,

It was late nearly lunch time as she got out of bed. She had another bad headache and she felt norse's and couldn't face any food. She noticed a mug beside her bed, funny don't remember making a drink last night. Must have only I don't remember much after getting near that old man in the Avenue.

Holding her head she felt sick and rushed into the bathroom and only just got her head over the toilet pan as she vomited the chewed up flesh she'd eaton last night. What the hell as she looked in the pan, what the fuck did I eat last night as I don't remember any of it as she noticed a bath towel laying on the floor, now what? Am I going mad I don't remember showering last night either. Then she thought maybe she'd eaton something bad at the race course stall. As the food stall's we're out in the heat. But that wouldn't make her forget things.

Maggie wanted her food and was making a noise, so she decided to try and put last night out of her mind for a while as she had a splitting headache. Walked in to the kitchen to get some food for Maggie, then washed the bad taste in her mouth with cold bottled water from the fridge before pouring her self a glass of pineapple juice then a couple of pills for her head. She felt stifled and needed air so walked to the front door and opened it and stood there sipping the juice. It was too hot outside to sit or even go out, so went over and put the local news on the television to see if everyone last nights got home safely after the music festival.

Then she suddenly remembered the old man walk behind her in Esplanade and wondered what happened to him, because that was when things went blank. Maybe I should go see a doctor, as I don't even know why? I'll have to ask Jason or next door she should know one, and the doctors office should be near here. Ye's that's what I'll do as this is the third time I have lost some hours of my life. Decided to lay on the couch and rest as her tummy was still upset and so far the pills hadn't worked on her head. Maggie decided to join her as curled up together and dozed off.

A few months had pasted since that last evening of Jazz Fest, and her memory lost. And for some reason she'd not gone to see a doctor as it had totally slipped her mind. Checking her morning emails before going to Jasons to help out, she realised that although the gigs had slowed some because of the heat and humidity in July which was terrible. She had a couple of emails from Clubs in Texas, that had been arrangements with Ruffin before he died. And as they had heard nothing from the new management, as time went bye they decided to contact her direct as they would like her and the band to play there Friday and Saturday for 1 hour each night between the 2 clubs. They had left a contact number to contact the clubs music arranger. Each club's email as she read them was nearly the same so maybe own by same person.

Summer couldn't believe it because right now her gigs barley covered the bills and rent. She couldn't wait to tell the boys straight away so got her mobile phone and phone Bryan to tell him the good news.

Bryan was busy cleaning his motorbike before the humidity go to bad to be outside, when his phone went. Glad to hear Summers voice, as he was going to phone her later about the band leaving town to find more work.

After 20 minutes on the phone he was relieve at her news. It meant they could stay in a cheap bed and breakfast for the 2 nights. Be worth it. This means we will have to shift the 2 gigs in Bywater and Treme in New Orleans. Two different times. Which they didn't mind in the least as the Clubs their were full of the wrong kind of locals. And she'd found it wasn't safe to walk so had to leave afterwards in a taxi, which meant a cut in the nights earnings.

Summer had laughter at the time telling Bryan she could take care of her self. But she still took the Taxi as the band had a van and lived know where near her. It's a shame the other place's in New Orleans rely on the tourist trade, which is from Feb too May so cut back on live gigs in the heat of the Summer months.

So Bryan it's okay for me to tell the Clubs in Austin and Houston that we would be happy to play their only we will have to work out the times for all the other clubs hoping we can get there and play before heading back as I have a solo gig at midnight on both days. I'll let you know when we will be off there after I'v worked out the dates and times, unless you would like to help me do it. Two heads are better than one and you know Texas and can work out the travel time's between each Club.

Bryan said he'd call around tomorrow late afternoon, by then you should have a reply. And hopefully we can be off Friday afternoon after fixing up cheap accommodation. God this is a win full, as we were all running out of money here.

Bryan I will make my own way back here by train as I have a gig back here at midnight on both day's. So no staying over, and in any case I couldn't afford to. I have to go as Im due at Jason's in half hour. See you all tomorrow. Then suddenly remembered Maggie, well girl I will still be able to buy your Tuna after all so no horrid wet cat food.

Jason was wondering if she was coming to help him decorate the bar area's main wall. And was about to phone her, when she came in to the bar.

After explaining about the emails then waited for him to reply.

Jason smiled I don't want you to go even if it is only for a few hour each day, I'll miss you baby. I have an old RV of Fathers, It works okay as I have been looking after it, altho mother wanted to sell it, only Father left it to me. In side it has a main bed at the back and a set of bunk bed's either side between the shower, toilet cubicle. Sleeps four with the main double. It'll do it good being used, and Father would wish it. Bryan and Paul your band members can drive it. So what do you say. Oh I'm not giving it to you just lending it each week to save you money on digs? Also your cat can live in it the two days.

Summer hugged him and kissed him on the lips which please as it solved a lot besides saved a lot for the guys. Only there is one thing Jason I'm coming back after the 9 o'clock gig which finish's at 10, Going to get a train back as I have a gig at the Casino here each evening at midnight on my own. I hope I can make it in two hours from there. She then went to step away from him, only he had got the wrong Idea and held her head and kissed her passionately, until he suddenly pulled away as his lip was bleeding badly. You didn't have to bit me looking at her horrified at what she did.

Holding a tissue at his lip he rushed into the back of the Bar to put a plaster on it, only when he took the bloody tissue away he saw a small hole in his lip so a plaster wouldn't do as it needed a stick.

He Came back out with a towel at his lip and asked Zain to take him to the emergence unit at the local Hospital. Looked towards her and said why baby? You must know I am in love with you and thought you were fond of me, I meant you know harm by the kiss then walked out to his car.

Leaving her stunned by what she'd just done. She couldn't understand how it happened as it wasn't on her mind at all.

To try and make a mend she got on with painting the feature wall hoping he'd not change his mind about the RV for the Guys.

After over three hours Jason came back with one stitch on his lip. And pain killers. Summer immediately said she was sorry, and quickly mention that he knew about her stepfather, I don't know what came over me I really am sorry and I am fond of you. You will just have to give us time. Jason looked at her then the finished wall and told her he forgave her, but won't be kissing her again without her permission.

Does it hurt that much as it was a tiny wound you could hardly see it she asked him?

What do you think? I won't be drinking hot coffee for a while? Summer thought men and pain. Then asked how she could make up for doing it?

You have done that all ready by doing the wall. Went in the back of the bar and came back with the RV's keys, come I'll show you over it. You're going to have to get one of the band to pick it up the day you leave. The RV was just as he said, and it had every thing you could want, it was perfect she told him and thankyou. I wouldn't have blamed you if you had changed your mind? Only I told you I'm coming back here Friday and Saturday. It will be very close on timing but I hope I can get back on the train in 1 hour 30 minutes allowing time to get to the Station and the taxi from the Station here.

I wouldn't do a thing like that to you baby and I'm glade your coming back each night. I have a feeling you are underestimating the time it takes from Texas to New Orleans by train, now baby it's well pasted lunch time, I don't know about you but I'm hungry so let's eat, forgetting his cut lip or pain as he called one of his staff to ask the chief if he could reheat the special meal that he had ordered as a surprise for her, and get a waitress to bring it in with the bottle of wine he'd got from the cellar. As he'd planned to tell her how he felt about her over the meal, but that had already happened.

Summer got a taxi for the short distance home after the meal. It was well into evening and starting to get dark now. Not many people about. She still couldn't understand why she bit him, and could only put it down to her childhood as the clouds opened up and it suddenly thundered then a flash of lighting as heavy rain fell as she climb into the Taxi.

Got it right for once on the news about the storm said the Taxi drive as sat inside wet from the short walk from the bar, and chatted on until he pulled up outside her place. Summer paid him and ran up the stairs and in doors socking wet even after a short distance, a flash of memory appeared in her head of her in the river suddenly happened for a split second then was gone. She tried to give it know he'd and went and changed in to a lounge outfit in the bathroom. Maggie kept away till she was dry. She then put music on as the storm got worse, made a coffee fed Maggie and put a dish of cat milk down and then phoned Bryan to tell him about the RV. Then she lay on the couch and watched a movie on prima on her cell phone as the dish was not working. Then the lights went so got her large table touch and waited the storm out. She didn't mind storms, there wasn't much that she was scared of as she looked at facebook on her table.

Three days later the band and herself were on the road to Texas in the RV. To their first gig at the Stabb's Club in Austin at 7 then travel to then travel to the other Club for the 9 o'clock gig. They would park up and all of them would be spending the night in the RV. As she found out it will take 9 hours 30 minutes to get by train to and back from gigs. So Maggie was with them and happy with a full belly and a warm bed. The litter tray was in the shower cubicle. That was the only down side for the boys as it meant the tray had to be taken out when they showered. Summer didn't mine in the least if it meant her cat could come.

The 4 gigs over the two nights were at The Stubb's Club, then The Moody theatre on the same night in Austin. Then the Continental Club in Houston on the next night, playing there twice on the same night only the second gig that night she played solo with her own music. All went better than well. The management were all great so was the money. And it would be a repeat every weekend. And all it cost them was the diesel for the RV between them. The gigs were so good that they'd give up the ropy 2 gigs back in New Orleans till the festival season next year. And Summer had managed to rearrange the gigs at the Casino so all was right with the world as they drove back home.

CHAPTER 6

It was well into 2025 and the festival season was on it's way again. Because the gigs in Texas were so good they had decided to just do the important gigs like the one in the French Quarter and then Race course. And Baton Rouge Louisiana Capital, they still had the Mardi Gras Ball although for some reason she wasn't happy about doing it if it wern't for the Mayor. And she'd now given up sing at Jasons Bar as well. The clientele in the clubs in Texas were wealthy patrons, so the band and herself were now in the up market Leigh.

It was now the very end of April and they were preparing for the last one Jazz fest in the French District, although the boys wern't keen on doing it, but promised to go by her judgment that it would help there band be know further than Texas. As people from all over the States come here for that Fest she told them. After there afternoon and evening playing that last day, they had enjoyed it and enjoyed the festivities there before and after in the Quarter.

Summer had one of her memory lost's again after it, she'd had a few but only when she was on her own and late at night and only in New Orleans. Which she thought strange and they were lasting longer? Also she had the bad heads each time. No more bruises, but she did have an outfit including shoes go missing after their last festival in the race course last year and now it was May she was getting worried about her memory.

Siting on her veranda that morning going though the memory loss and strange things that had been happening to her, she'd started taking notes. And right now she had a feeling she might have a tumour in her head, as that would give her memory loss's so the medical notes about tunas had read on line.

Maggie was sitting at the door, that was as far as she ever went now. And watched her talking to herself. Summer looked at her sitting there and told her not to worry about her talking to herself. Because I'm going to make an appointment at the doctor for this afternoon if possible, taking out her cell phone and dial the number her neighbour had given her the other day.

A receptionist on the other end told her that she could see the doctor at 4pm.

Only after Summer had told her why she needed to be seen that day. She believed she had a tumour because she had long blackouts. Other wise she'd have had to wait a couple of days. And herself and the band would be in Texas then. Maybe now I will find out why and get some peace if and when they cure it she told Maggie. Now girl I think i'll have a long cold shower and get dressed even out here in the early morning it's humid for May. At least in Texas it is only hot not humid as well.

Outside the doctors which was a brick building unlike all the wooden houses in the area she noticed. It looked modern as she walked inside into a hallway then through a glass door into reception with a dozen or so chairs around the walls door. Walked up to reception and said who she was and that she had an appointment for 4.

The young blonde receptionist told her to go and wait on a chair and she will be called when doctor was free.

After what seemed like hours to her, was only 34 minutes as she looked at her cell phone as she was called. After giving the doctor her medical history, which she'd made up. He got started asking why she was there? Then when she told him, he checked her eyes and felt her head took her pulse and said he couldn't find any thing wrong with her. But to be on the safe side he'd send her for a Cat scan at the hospital. He told her it would take about a week before they sent her an appointment as they were very busy "as he was". Give your details and cellphone number and email also your medical insurance details. You do have medical insurance Miss?

Of course doctor and thankyou, he then got on with writing up her notes on a form and looked up and said sharply good bye.

She didn't feel like going home, so decided to go to Jason's as she needed a friendly face to talk to. He knew about the blackout, so maybe he'll come with her to the hospital when she got the appointment just in case it was a tumour or even Cancer. As it had to be something?

A week went by, with the band and herself doing their usual trip to Texas, now home she'd still not had her appointment for the cat scan as she checked her emails daily on her phone. They did have an email from a Club in LA, word of them had spread further, and the club management at Hyde Sunset wondered if they could come for an interview to see if they played the kind of music that the club hired. Summer couldn't believe it and reached for her cell phone disturbing Maggie who was on her lap, so the cat jumped off.

Bryan answered his phone while busying himself cleaning his pressures motorbike, his pride and joy.

Hi Summer, what's on your mind as I only saw you yesterday?

A club in Los Angeles is asking for us to try out at their Club. Do you know what that means for us if we get the gig in LA, we have hit the big time and New Yorks Madison Square Gardens here we come? "The up coming Cat scan had gone complete out of her head".

Bryan asked the name of the Club?

Hyde Sunset in Hollywood area she told him.

I'll check and see on line he told her, to see what sought of club it is, as it's a long way to go for just for one gig. I'll let you know as soon as I'v checked it out.You realise we would have to move the clubs in Texas around, might even cut one he told her?

Didn't think about that but it might be worth it. I'm going o check the club out as well. Just a thought why don't I send them one of our DVD's we had done to sell at the clubs in Texas? It will save us the drive up there Bryan?

Good idea should have thought about that first. Send them an email to let them know. I'll not tell the others till we hear back.

Summer went on line and looked up the club, and it was good, then decided to look up other clubs in LA. After all no harm in trying.

After and hour she'd looked up 3 to start with and wrote covering letters and a DVD of them playing something also her email address which she was use to doing since school as her friends use text or email all the time as everyone did now days. Luckily she had a pad and pen to write down the address's of the clubs and she had several large brown envelopes she'd bought to send back something she'd bought on line that was broken. She was glad she'd kept them as she put the four letters and DVD'S in each one and wrote her address on the back. Now all she had to do was go to the main post office and post them off, after rechecking each address was correct.

Maggie I'll pick you up some fresh fish as I am going near the main food market near the Post Office.I'll also pick up some fresh fruit. I'm sure you under stand me old girl. Picking up her shoulder bag checked the envelopes again and put them inside then left.

On the long walk to the Post Office in the heat she thought about what it meant if they only got 2 clubs hiring them. She'd be able to buy that red shopping scooter she had seen on line. It was Japanese and came with spare parts. A firm some where in the States sold them from Japan. She could use it for all sought of things. Even travel out of town. At the Post Office she kissed each one then crossed her fingers as she gave them in over the counter to be recorded delivery and paid with her visa card.

Outside she took a deep breath and hoped something good would come by the DVDS. Crossed the road and walked around the open air market stalls run by Vietnamese women, and bought a lot of fresh veg and fish also fruit. At a stool she got a cool drink as it was deadly in the heat. But if you gave into the heat, she felt you'd only go out at night after 8. Looking at her two bags of fish and produce she realised she'd over bought as she slowly took the long walk back home.

Once back indoors she took the fish off the top of one of the bags and put it in the fridge, then went into the bathroom stripped off and stood under the cold shower before putting the shopping away. She was bloody glad they had air conditioning one of the reasons she took the place.

Four days later while at Jasons going though his books as he was worried about money as he had been only opened Thursday, Friday and Saturday and Sunday after 9pm.

And the sales of food were way down. He had his mothers money that was really his she'd stole from sales. But it was not enough.

Summer turned and looked at the worried face and told Jason that she had a plan to help him get more punters in to drink, and open from Wednesday. Put in air conditioning in stead of the fans in the ceiling every where. And offer cold beer and ice-cold fruity cocktails. You can afford it just, and it will pay for its self in the long run. What do you say?

It was so simple why hadn't he thought of it as he liked the idea.

I even have a firm on line here who can come in and do it in 2 days, what do you say Jason?

How much is it going to cost me?
1500 hundred dollars to put it in ever room all but the bathrooms and cellar. Thats the guesthouse, restaurant and here so what do you say?

Go ahead and hire them baby, if you're sure of the price. I have money from mother that will cover it and some. I was saving it for emergencies and this is giving her a big hug, he'd liked to have kissed her but remembered last time rubbing his lip.

Summer walked home happy she could help Jason out. Even after 2 years in charge he still had a lot to learn with the business. Funny she thought he always turned to her for help, although she'd never run a business and he was older than her by 4 years. In fact she had managed her life well considering she'd come there at 15 nearly 16. It was as if she were a lot older and world wise, which she felt she wasn't.

It was 3 weeks into June and nothing from the hospital, but good news from the Clubs in Los Angeles. So the scan went to the back of her mind again.

The DVD's paid off on three of the clubs, she couldn't believe it and phoned Bryan with the news. The Poppy night Club is one she told him, it is a high class members only place. Set in a private house in 2 private rooms with a luxurious, exclusive bar and lounge. The Club that contacted her on email first The Hyde Sunset also plus OHM

Nightclub was interested, they have a spacious dance room and 150 LED panels that project an interesting glow in the space we would play Bryan.

How the hell did you get the other 2, you never said anything about them Bryan replied excited at the prospect.

I sent four DVD's off to the four others as well, hoping to get good news. Three want to see us to disguise contracts and money. You know what this means we might have to move there if all goes well as it is too far to travel there and back each week.

Bryan told her to wait and see first after we have visiting the clubs before we decide. So when do you think we should go, only it will have to be soon as we will have the Texas gigs to do? Luckily we aren't under contract to any there.

I could email the 3 Clubs straight away Bryan and tell them we could be there day after tomorrow. As it will take about 19 hours to travel to LA in the RV. And we will need to stop for a few hours for Paul to rest so add that on. What do you say?

Great I'll phone the boys and tell them, and we can leave around 4 am tomorrow before the heavy traffic. I could meet you at Jasons in an hour to pick up the RV with Paul, shame he is the only one with a driving license to drive it. Do you think he'll let us still use it as it might mean we all move, and we all know he is keen on you?

We'll not tell him till we know. Then hire the RV as a rental like any car retail, after all he cain't drive it and it was just gathering dust and cobwebs when we first saw it.

Fine Summer see you in an hour, that will give you time to make up a story to tell Jason why we need it before we arrive.

All went okay with Jason, as he was very busy now with many more punters after the air conditioner was installed and the change with cold drinks now.

Summer and Maggie were at the back lying on the bed as they set off for Los Angeles, the boys were sitting talking away excited at the prospect of playing in tinsel town.

The time was 11am as they drove into Los Angeles Little Venice on the Pacific coast Highway, and set about finding a car park they that would take their RV. Then some where cheap to stay over for 3 nights.

On Little Venice beach were body builders surrounded by young collage girls watching. Shawn got out and asked one of the young men if he knew where there was some where cheap to stay for a couple of days with a large carpark?

The young man couldn't take his eyes of Summer who was standing by the RV. And didn't once look at Shawn told him Samesum Hostel not far from here. Is she your's pointing to Summer.

No, we are here to play at some clubs if its any of your business. Whats the address of this Hostel?

No offence, so keep your shirt on man. It's in Windway Avenue just up that short road and turn right can't miss it.

Shawn thanked him and went back to the RV and told the guys. Summer was not keen on the Hostel as it meant sharing with them, so decided to sleep in the RV with Maggie.

After booking in to the Hostel they were shown to a dorm, which the boys thought was good and clean for 35 dollars a night. They were told they had two private rooms with bathroom for 95 dollars a night.The guys knew Summer would't pay that so declined the room.

After they all walked around looking for some where cheap to eat or a takeaway, they saw a Mexican joint had a queueing outside so they agreed it must be good so joined the end of it.

They all bought the same a Mexican sandwich piled high inside with black bean paste and avocado, onion and chicken, it was cheap and tasty and then they sat on the beach and eat it, washing it down with a cold coke in the warm sun "no humidity like New Orleans" So it made a change to eat outside at just gone 12 mid-day. Their first appointment was at 4pm that day.

Tomorrow the other two were at 11am and 4pm, so they hoped to leave LA straight after.

Until their first appointment they decided to become tourist and took a bus to Beverley Hills and got of just before Rodeo drive steps. Walked around some of the Expensive shops in tree lined roads, then off to Hollywood walk of fame and walked along looking at some of the stars in that section, some star's we're of new actors along Hollywood Boulevard by the Chinese theatre there.

Summer looked at her phone it said 3 25 pm so they would have to get a taxi as they didn't want to be late for their first appointment which was in the Bel-Air ritzy neighbourhood.

Bel-Air was even posher than Beverly Hills. And set in the residential enclave of the verdant Foothills of Santa Monica Mountains and was very impressive with it's grand houses.

The taxi arrived at the entrance gates of Sunset Boulevard, which lead to winding streets lined with bigger Lavish Mansions on Large properties and also the entertainment industry area. They drove past a sign which said elite exclusive Bel-Air Country Club, members only. Then further on they pulled up in front of two wrought iron gates with a monitor on one of the concrete pillars that were either side. The taxi man lend out and pressed the speaker and gave Summers full name plus the band's. The gates automatically opened and the taxi drove through the gates and up the winding drive to a massive house painted white with large Roman pillars out front and above on the pillars a balcony. They stood in ore.

Waiting at the top of the drive was a well dressed tall slim coloured man who looked very impressive. Bryan paid the taxi trying not to cringe at the cost as he could have eaton for a week on it.

Summer got out first from the front seat then the four guys who had been crammed into the back of the taxi managed to get out dignified.

They were escorted in to the mansion and through a corridor in to the Private Club at the back leading out onto the grounds and pool which from the french doors looked big so she thought, and she started to get nerves as the place looked a million dollars in its gold and silver and pink decor.

Please wait here the man said pointing to several french chairs which looked uncomfortable, they looked more like flimsy dinning chairs so she felt, so stood while the boys sat.

A middle aged suave looking sophisticated tall slim stylish white gentleman dress causally in expensive clothes and gold watch, bracelet and thin gold chain came though a door at the side an introduced himself as Daniel Moura I am the owner.

You look as beautiful as you looked in your DVD Miss Dala Rosa and your band are presentable, so you should go down well here pointing to a small stage. I liked your music, you have a lovely voice young lady. I am glad you have bought some instruments. We have drummers and a piano as you can see. So why don't you sing and play something for me and 2 of my management. Pulling a cord hanging by the french doors which were hung with heavy beautiful curtains tied up each side. Two men dressed in dark suits and ties reminded Summer of Gangsters by the way they looked and held them selves came in. If you wouldn't mind getting started as she stood staring at the men. Summer and the guys quickly turned and walked to the stage and got ready.

After 20 minutes they'd finished playing.
One of the managers walked towards her and told her he enjoyed her singing and piano playing. Then introduced himself as head of security for the whole property.
Mr Moure also told her that she was even better singing in person, and that if they can come to terms on how much for 2 nights then they had a deal. So let's talk business all of you?

After a while they all agreed on money which was double an hour from what they got in Texas let alone New Orleans. And the hours of play were midnight till one, twice a week. Maybe more if they went down well with the rich clientele.

Summer and the guys left the Mansion Club on a hire, and drove to the beach for a swim before the boys change for dinner and a night out at a club. Summer took Maggie for a walk on a harness on a large patch of grass with several Palm trees for her to use as scratch pads instead. of going with the boys. Poor Maggie would be shut up for a while in the RV, while they played over the three nights but at least she'd have her to curl up to at night. Maggie hated the harness and was happy just lying on the bed in the RV and her Tuna in stead, but she couldn't tell Summer only pull on the harness, then she sat and wouldn't move. Summer had to pick up Maggie and take her back to the RV.

The evening in Los Angeles was full of music cocktails and dancing for them. Even Summer who didn't drink normally had found an English Pub with music just of the beach right near the carpark. But that night she wasn't her usual self, luckily the boys wern't there to noticed. She was completely out of character and enjoyed the being in the Pub drinking.

Next morning Summer woke with a blinding headache, and found herself still fully clothed laying on the bed. The outfit was not what she remembered wearing earlier last night, and realised she had another memory loss. Then remembered her Cat scan she was waiting for. If the hospital send it by post while she's away, they will think she changed her mind. Not a lot she can do about it now dam it, as the guys and herself were off to another appointment at a club in a couple of hours at 11 30 am getting up to get showered and ready.

OHM Nightclub was just that, full of coloured fairy lights inside and 150 led panels that projected an interested glow in the dance space. And everything went more or less the same as the other appointment, and again they would also play over 2 nights 9 till 11 given them enough time to get to the other gig at midnight. Money was more which made it worth putting up with the lights.

They still had the other appointment at 4pm Hyde Sunset Club and hoped it would be more subdued.
As they entered the Club it was full of dim red lights every where, making it very secluded when you sat in a booth against the wall. Friday evening 2 till 3 am that way they could do all the gigs. They will bring Shawn's old Van to get around in as well as the RV.

The guys and herself sat and disguised about getting to all the gigs in Texas which was next door. Also about moving there for half a week and spend the rest in New Orleans. Or giving New Orleans up, which Summer said she'd not do as it was her home now.
So after a lot of talking decided to rent a house for all of them to stay in while they stayed in LA. In Little Venice, they could all chip in to the deposit

and rent. Tomorrow before leaving we should line up a place. As the gigs are next week, and the contracts are for 4 months renewable. That evening she decided to go with them to an English Pub in a street off the Coastal Road in Santa Monica, that way she won't get a headache and have a memory loss after, also no drink as she was sure they would do fruit juice like other Pubs. She had no memory of being there the night before.

After a couple of hours at the Pub Summer had done a lot of thinking and decided to tell the guys that she would stay in the RV From Friday till Sunday, then drive back to New Orleans for the rest of the time as LA was not really a City she'd like to spend to much time in as she wasn't one of the rich folk. And Little Venice was not her idea of some where to live other wise she'd have gone there first in stead of New Orleans. Also she'd heard there were thousands of homeless people not far from Little Venice which upset her because of the rich side of Los Angeles.

Bryan and the others wern't pleased at her news and told her so. And tried to talk her out of it. I didn't think you could drive?
I learned at 13 on my grandpa's Ranch during my school holiday's. "which was true" You can't drive the RV Summer as   surly it is too big for you to handle?

Jason gave me lessons in the RV so I could take my test in it. And I past first time, I didn't tell you lot as I saw know reason. I have been saving up for a scooter to use in New Orleans.
Remember one thing it is my voice there are paying for, and I have know intention of letting you down here in LA, remember one thing also that the new gigs were my Idea and I was the one did all the paper work for them. Her words hurt.
Paul was disappointed that she wouldn't be sharing their digs together but that was all. He

sought of fancied her. The other two said nothing. Leaving Bryan hated what she had said but gave in as there was nothing they could say to change her mind. They guys did agree among them selves that they would move out their, so would start to look for a flat or house to rent before going back home to pack up their things. Which would mean she'd have to wait till tomorrow night for them all to leave to go back to New Orleans.

CHAPTER 7

It was the end of June and Summer and the Guys were playing their first gig in the Private Poppy club in Bel Air. Mr Moura greeted them at the club doors before getting one of his waiters to show them to the back room to get ready to preform on Stage.

In the Clubs lounge room they could see famous film stars enjoying dancing on the dance floor, also some sitting chatting among them selves. I'm nerves she said, as I'v never played in front of film stars. Powerful business men yes, she suddenly felt light headed and had to sit for a few minutes before going on.

The clientele in the room stopped what they were doing when the band started and Summer started singing. Making Mr Moura pleased he'd hired them. The evening was a great success on all their parts as the evening drew to a close.

Saturday morning came around and Summer was in the RV in the front garden of the guys rental which was handy for her. Only again she awoke with a headache and hang over and a nasty taste in her mouth, something she had no recollection of as she lay there. The bang on the RV's door went though her like a knife as she got up to see what the guys wanted at this hour.

Bryan stood outside in shorts and t shirt. You must have had a good night last night, as it's gone midday. We thought you were never getting up. How was it with Graig Douglas "movie star"?

What do you mean I came straight back here after the gig and fed Maggie?

You must have had a lot to drink if you don'T remember that you went out with him in his red sports car afterwards. You really must have been plastered if you can't remember anything.

I have I have a slight hang over I believe, as I'v never had one before plus a terrible headache. I must feed my cat then shower and dress, so if you don't mind leaving me. I won't be more than half an hour, then I'll need coffee and pancakes from Daisy's kitchen if you don't mind coming with me?

The rest of the guys are on the beach told me to get you. So I'll wait while you do what you have to as he sat on the steps of the house in the sun.

As she got showered and dressed she tried hard to remember what happened after the gig, but she couldn't. How could she get in a car with this Craig who ever and not remember it, that's impossible surely so what the hell is happening to me? She must find out about the Cat scan when she got back to New Orleans and find out why she'd not had an appointment for it. It was more important than ever now to find out what is going on in her head.

The rest of her time in Los Angels, the same thing happened to her. She found herself the morning after in a strange bed naked next to a strange guy. She slowly got out of bed without waking him, and collected all her clothes off the floor where they were strewn and went into the bathroom and got dressed. This can't be happening to me not again it's not possible, but it was?

The bathroom had a large window in it, so rather than go back in the bedroom, then walk though the house to get to the front door. She went over to look out the open window to see if she could climb down, and yes there was a thick vine climbing over the wall of the back of the house and down the side of a Sunroom. And below was the roof of the sunroom. Making it easy to get down to then climb down into there garden which was very big and green she noticed. So taking a deep breath she climb out and down onto the roof, then down the vine to the ground, quickly looked for a way out of the garden.

Two Rockefeller came bounding round the corner of the house growling ready to bite the intruder in the garden. Summer froze as the dogs saw her and ran up to her. They walked around her a dozen times as she slowly guided the two of them to a side gate an inch at a time.

The dogs for some reason didn't bite her or even jump up, in fact they stopped circling her and sniffed her then walked beside her. It seemed they liked her. She'd always wanted a dog but her Stepfather wouldn't allow her to have one. More than likely she was scared the dog would turn on him if he tried to rape she thought as the gate got nearer.
Summer took the opportunity to speak softly to them and they seemed to like it. Slowly she put her hand out and touched one of them on the forehead then the other. For some reason they liked her smell which meant she could continue to walk to the side gate and get away.

At the gate she stroked the dogs still talking to them, then opened the gate and walked out into a side driveway and closed the gate behind her. Keeping to the high hedge she walked down onto the road and then took off as fast as she could out of the area till she came to some large maned security gates, nervously walked up to the gates and stood waiting for one of the two men to open them. A small gate at the side of the large pair was opened for her, she turned thanked the men and walked though it in to Beverley Hills.

Feeling relieved that She'd now left Bel Air. Walked slowly hoping she was going in the right direction to get out of there walking down hill. She saw a cab on the other side of the road coming towards her and hail it. Got in and gave the boys address in Venice. Sat back and tried hard to remember what happened last night.

It looked like every one in the area we're still asleep, including the guys. Looked at her watch for the first time that morning and saw it was just gone 5am. Paid the cab and went in to her RV. Maggie was all over her as she'd been away all night. Summer stroked her then got her a meal of Tuna after getting two headache pills and switching on the coffee machine.

Looking at Maggie eating she told her they were leaving right now and going home instead of later this evening.

They would be back hopefully early to morrow morning. Taking the pills with a sip of hot coffee she then put it on the dashboard as she sat in front of the engine. She'd not showered or cleaned her teeth even her long hair must have looked a mess and she most likely smelt but I have to get out of this City she told Maggie, so Here goes nothing old girl, this will be my first long haul drive 18 hours with an hour in the middle to get cleaned up and food I'd say around 20 hours before home. God that has a nice sound.

I'll phone the guys on my food stop miles away. I have to have that Cat Scan in New Orleans or I'll go mad not knowing what is happening to me.

Summer was relieved to see the sign for New Orleans in the distance 11 miles it read.

She crossed the river in to New Orleans and never felt so happy and relieved that they got there in one piece. The guys will get over not having her there full time as she drove in the silent empty darkness along the main roads to her area. Street Parked the RV outside her place and picked up Maggie and went up into her place to sleep after that long drive. It was 4 37 am as she climb into bed with Maggie on top of her and went into a deep sleep.

The sun shone though the window onto the bed awaking Maggie up. So she walked over Summer's body till she woke.

The hot sun was streaming though the curtains but it was cool inside with the air conditioning. Stretched and reached for her cell phone. The time was 11 43 am she'd slept soundly no night mares or headache thankfully. Got up and walked into the kitchen and put coffee on then fed Maggie, cleaned out her litter tray then took her coffee into the bedroom, and went and had a shower and got dressed. Took her phone and phoned the Hospital to check on the Cat scan appointment and sat on the bed and waited to speak to someone.

After a second or two she was told that she's canceled it weeks back.

Summer said they must be mistaken as she never phoned them since visiting the hospital the first time. After a lot of to-ing and fro-ing, she was told that they could fit her in today at 4pm. Summer thanked her and said she'd be there.

She then phoned Jason who was pleased that she was back in town, and said of course he'd take her to the Hospital. Come for lunch first before we go to the Hospital?

Summer thanked him and said she would be there in 20 minutes as she had a lot to tell him. Put fresh water and dried cat food down and left on the air conditioning, kissed Maggie and said she'd be back before evening as she was going to spent the evening sitting on her veranda relaxing with soft music.

At Jason she decided to leave out waking up naked beside an unknown guy. And just tell Jason she had two memory looses. She knew she had been raped the second night. Stands to reason she told herself she was naked.

The streets in Frenchman were full of Students enjoying the music from the clubs there, as she walked through to the Balcony bar and guesthouse and restaurant in lower Royal Street.

The heat had been unbearable as she walked. But once inside the Bar it was cool. Jason was chatting to some girls by the bar when he saw her and his face light up. Hi babe it's good to see you back. I thought you might decided to stay there permanently?

The guys are but not me, I drove your RV all the way back on my own. I don't think I would have been able if it had been one of those bigger RV's. I also slept in it, the guys found a cheap house to rent in Venice. Maggie's happy to be back as well.

That bloody Cat? Giving her a funny look.

Ye's the cat Maggie, why so nasty? She's my family.

Come on Summer really? Now baby let have lunch as we don't have long before we have to leave.

The light meal was nice as was the fruit juice he'd layed on for her. As she sat and eat, she told him about the two more memory looses. One where she'd spent the night after the gig clubbing and drinking which she had know memory of. The guys told her the next day. The second she found her self some where strange after the gig hours later. Both times she had the bad Head pains. I think I am going mad Jason. Then I phoned the Hospital this morning and they said I'd canceled my appointment. Luckily they did have a cancelation at 4.

Jason could say nothing about her memory looses that would explain them, so said nothing. Only that they should leave soon for the hospital.

Summer nervously got into his car and they drove to the Hospital.

On arrival she stood looking at the building nervously. Jason put his arm around her shoulders and walked her inside to the reception decked. Summer gave her name and waited then a nurse came out of a room and called her name.

In the room stood the large machine as she sat down near it to answer some questions. It looked frightening as she couldn't take her eyes off it. Then she was asked to take off any jewellery, then to lye down and keep completely still. After a couple of minutes or so it was over and she was taken outside to the monitors where the doctor was looking at the scan of her brain.

Summer stood waiting to hear the worst only to be told that they was nothing wrong with her head. He even pointed it out to her so she could see for her self. So why the memory loose and its getting worse. I awoke this morning in a strangers bed when I thought I had gone back to where I was staying. And the headaches what about them?

You do have an unusual brain pattern miss. You need to see a Neurologist I will arrange it for you if you wish?

Ye's please as I feel I am going mad doctor.

I wouldn't say that miss, there has to be a reason for your memory looses I'm sure. You'r get your new appointment at the deck on the way out.

Outside Jason asked her how did it go?

It didn't I have to see another doctor. She'd not tell him what kind yet as she felt embarrassed. Paid with her medical insurance then got her new appointment Thursday morning. Which meant her and Maggie would have to fly to LA for Thursdays gigs and sleep on the coach at the guys place because of Maggie, as there was no way she could leave her in a hotel room while she worked because of her litter tray. She'd have to let the guys know as well. It meant added expense with the plane but what the hell her health was more important.

To her surprise when on the way back to her place she told him her planes, he offered to drive the RV to LA and fly back. So she'd have the RV to stay in. You know how I feel about you babe, I'd do anything for you, know that don't you?

Summer kissed him on his lips and thanked him, I'll pay your air fare.

Know you won't babe I'm doing okay now thanks to you so I'm happy to pay. You can sing for the customers tomorrow night if you want to?

I'd love to and thanks.

The three days in New Orleans went quickly for her, and today Thursday Jason was driving the RV back to LA after going with her to the Hospital that morning. He'd be flying back as she flew out Friday.

It had been a funny two evenings for her, as it seemed she'd spent each evening enjoying herself, not that she could remember any of it If it hadn't been for Jason relaying what happen the night before not realising she had know memory of it. Except for the first evening as she went over things after the Scan.

Now she was sitting with Jason in the neurologists waiting room that Friday morning. She had phoned the guys to say that she might be late today as she would be flying back, and have to go straight to the Club, she'd let them know nearer the gig's time. She told Bryan she had a doctors appointment she couldn't miss.

The waiting room had a couple of other people waiting, but she noticed that there were three doctors at that clinic so wasn't worried about having to wait long as they sat in silence together.

A distinguish looking gentleman wearing a white coat came out of a door in the back with a young patient. Then they parted at reception and the distinguish man went back in his room for a couple of minutes then came out and asked if a Summer Dalla-Rosa was in there?

Summer nervously said here sir and got up. The doctor introduced himself as Dr Micheal Novikov and led her into his consulted room, and asked her to sit. After writing something on a form he filed it in a cupboard sat and faced her and asked her what she thought was wrong with her head, as he'd read her notes from the other doctor and had a good Idea what could be wrong, although he'd not met many patients with it in his time.

Summer showed him the new bruise she'd woken up with that morning and had know Idea how she got them and this wasn't the first time as it is happening a lot. And told him all the things that have happened to her and how many time she'd lost her memory and woke up dressed different or somewhere else.

He asked when it first started to happen?

When I first came to live here in the year 22. I was 17 so it's been going on for over 3 years. It never happened where I lived before.

Did some damaging emotional trauma or abusive experience happen in your childhood?

Summer asked if she told the doctor could he tell any one her story?

No what you say will stay with me I promise. As I am not aloud to tell any one with your say so. If it did happen then that could be your trigger?

I was abused by my stepfather. And in the end I ran away from home because of it.

That could be the trigger. It will take therapy over a period of time. And if you will let me I would like to hypnotise you later on in our sections what do you say?

I will have to think about it doctor.

Thats fine, but I would like to see you again so your next appointment is Monday week about this time as the sooner we start the better, what do you say?

Make it Wednesday as I work in Los Angeles Friday and Saturday.

Fine each Wednesday until your memory comes back. I want you to keep a note book on the dates and how long your loose memory last. And any side effect like the first time you told me about. As it sounds like you could also have symptoms of violent behaviour contrasting with your normal personality?

Summer said she'd kept notes already and would bring them with her next time she see him on Wednesday. So what is wrong with me?

I believe you have what's known as personality disorder, the signs and symptoms make it look that way. I'll know better further into your sections and if you let me Hypnotise you Miss I'll know sooner. Now I'm sorry but I have another patient waiting. Let me know miss about hypnotising you soon.

Summer couldn't believe what he had said, Only would go along with it, if only to see if it was that or something else, as she thanked him and got up and walked over to the door. The doctor opened it and followed her out to greet the new patient.

So how was it babe, you don't look as if he has helped you by your face?

There was no way she was going to tell Jason what the doctor had said, so lied to him telling him that her brain was tied with all that had happened to her in the last 3 years being so young. The doctor is going to see me next

Wednesday and each one till he has help sort me out.

Is that all the doctor said? Doesn't seems correct when you think of your memory loose's.

Remember I saw a different side of you when you lost your memory. It was as if you were a different person all together Summer?

Summer said nothing in reply just walked to his car and stood waiting to get in it. Then all the way back to her place she sat in silence. There was no way she even believed what the doctor had said.

There was know way she had another personality inside her. She just couldn't believe it no way?

Back in Los Angeles late Friday, she changed in the plane toilet and got a taxi to the first gig, where the guys were waiting for her. She'd put what the doctor and what Jason had said out of her mind and get on with her life in LA.

The guys were relieved to see her, because without her they had nothing as she was the heart of the band.

Summer got straight into the first song, relieved to see the place was full. Her good voice had got around. And they had sold quite a lot of DVD's at the 3 Clubs in LA. So much so that the boys had found a studio in LA down town that would do CD's for them after hearing their music. And was happy to add them on their label.

It seemed a lot had happened in both places she realised. Now with a music label they were moving on up higher in the music business.

The guys told her that they had got 3 new gigs, one for lunchtime on a Saturday and Sunday Bunch time at a famous LA top Hotel. The Beverly Hills Hotel, a Dorchester collection Paul told her. The other at a new Club that had just opened a few weeks before, for Sunday evening which pleased her as it meant the guys were getting gigs without her.

That night after their gig the guy's we're going to enjoy them selves at another Club, and asked Summer to join them like last time.

Summer told them she was third after along drive back and was going to bed, hoping Jason had arrived outside their place with the RV, as he was going to phone me but hasn't yet?

At the guy's place there was not sign of Jason so phoned him. He was on the outskirts of LA and would be with her soon, only he'd missed his plane back. Traffic was bad baby all the way here. So if you don't mind I'll have to stay the night and fly out in the morning, I managed to get a transfer to tomorrow. Hope you know somewhere I can get a good big takeaway as I haven't stops since New Orleans baby.

Of cause you can stay and I'll pop and get a takeaway for you, as there is a good one near here, be back before you arrive.

Jason arrived tired and relieved to be there. Telling her that there was major accident out side Houston which closed the road for over 2 hours.

She collected the Cat and her things from the house and the food and walked towards the RV. Jason had taken the food from her and dived back inside the RV as he was starving as he'd had nothing but mints and coffee since leaving.

Summer was pleased to be back in the RV as was Maggie who ran to the bed at the back of it and curled up and went to sleep.

Glad to see your cat is happy to see me,

You'v not welcomed me with a kiss, Or said anything?

Sorry Jason only I'm tired like you. I'm glad you wern't in that crash, sitting next to him and started to help herself to some of the food as there was no food on the plane and she also hadn't't eaton at

Jason's bar. Only she'd been so busy that it had slipped her mind. After food Jason showered and put clean clothes on and they both went to bed, him on the bunk and herself with Maggie, as Jason was to tired to care where he slept. Any other time he'd slept beside herself and kicked the cat off the queen size bed at the back as he fell asleep.

The next morning she woke at 9 17am with a headache and found Maggie a sleep on top of her, which was as it was last night. Got up and made Maggie food, while a happy Jason who'd been up an hour and was dressed as he had to leave in a few minutes for the Airport and was waiting for the Taxi. Coffee will be stewed as It's been made a while babe. I have to leave soon but I'll keep in touch on my tablet via the video on text. Was a great night baby thanks to you, you were beautiful.

Before she could ask what he meant the taxi pulled up and Jason kissed her passionately and left saying as he went, be good babe we'll take up were we left off back home.

She stood wondering what the hell he meant take up where they left off, as she looked at Maggie. Put the coffee on and looked out at the guys rental house no one was up. She didn't want to stay outside the Guys rental last night but as it was late when Jason got to LA it was easier. Now it was daylight she could navigate the streets with the large vehicle and find some where else to park that was near open land to walk the cat on her harness. Poured out a coffee and got a muffin and went to the outside door to sit outside in the sun and eat before showering. And before the noise of the four guys when they get up. Still wondering what Jason meant by his words. She'd ask him in person Monday. As her head ached, God please not again, it can't be I just don't believe it not with

Jason here. Turned and went back and sat at the front of the RV.

She knew something had happened to her but what last night? Finished her coffee and went back inside to put some music on to relax her, showered and got ready to drive away from the guys place in south Los Angeles, to find a place in a carpark along the beach in Santa Monica.

Once there she for a carpark she could stay at for a large fee for the three days, and parked up and saw to Maggie putting fresh water and dried food done and got out of the Van.

Walked up to the road to get a taxi to the guys place in a circle all look alike small attached brick houses in a cul-de-sac, with a pool and several palm trees around making it look a lot less like a complex with its large pool further behind several more houses as well. She'd not really looked at it till now.

Cost the guys a fair bit, being a complex it had security which they liked as LA had thousands of homeless people not all nice beside a large criminal element. Seattle were she came from or New Orleans hadn't anything like it. Not that she would like to live there full time. It was more an estate for the movie industry's young workers in their studio's, not for families.

Bryan and Paul came out to meet her, glad you've moved out of our carpark as management don't allow large vehicles here or animal, only you were here parked up last night and several nights before that.They contacted us yesterday about your RV, as it was only to be temporary. Oh by the way there was a terrible murder last weekend here in Hollywood.

This is LA surely there are murders a lot here, like New Orleans she replied? So what's special about this one? I was thinking of buying a gun my self when I got back to New Orleans.

This was no gun shooting, the poor guy was bitten to death on his face and neck and bleed to death Bryan told her. A famous Actor, they haven't given out his name yet only that he drove a red Ferrari which was found miles away Little Venice on the beach burnt out.

Now how do you know that guys, I mean they don't normally give out the details of how, for a while if ever. They don't here in New Orleans as far as I know she said?

Shawn was the one who found the guy on the beach hidden behind some big rocks last night late. He went to piss near it, and saw a dismembered foot sticker out, and told the rest of us, so you could say we all saw the body. He'd been there a week in that heat the flies were every where and the seagulls, who must have dislodged it from where it had been hidden as the heat made him smell, never seen a dead body before, quite exciting.

So what happened to you that Saturday night it happened. After the gig you went back to the RV then not long after you turned up at Club Mayan where you knew we'd be. Then stayed for an hour, you said you were going outside the club to get some air and never came back? We thought you were enjoying your self dancing and drinking with us. Paul went outside to see if you were okay, no sign of you in the area Summer.

Summer quickly made up a lie, I got a cab and went back to the RV as I was feeling a little sick from the drink and dancing, after all I'm not use to it am I guys? "she remembered nothing of that night".Why ask me now as it's been a week?

Wondered if you had seen anything that night on the beach when you walked the cat that was all. Next time you disappear let us know with a killer around.

I'll do just that guys, now let's go for a swim in your pool, after all you pay enough for the up keep? Her head ache had long gone and she was feeling her old self.

The two gigs at different Clubs went well, and she went out with the guys afterwards, she was scared she'd go back to the RV to rest and find she'd gone out again. She so wanted not to believe that, but realised it was true that she'd somehow blackout or something as she lost her memory for at least 2 or 3 hours then wake up in the morning without knowing anything. And that time she'd got bruises. So she might as well go out with them straight after the last gig. Many places were still open at 1am till 4 am so they could relax and enjoy them selves.

Only she knew that was not the reason for going with the guys. She was scared to be along after a gig in her RV. Maggie couldn't talk and tell her that she was changing to this other self if that was what happened to her. How the hell could she find out if it really happened to her or there was some other underline reason know one knew a bout Yet?

That Sunday day after the new brunch gig She drove back to New Orleans around 7pm. She couldn't wait to get back and go on line and look up Identity disorder and see if she could find out if there was much research on the subject, also if there could be another reason researchers had found that course memory loose.

Her laptop was back in her house in New Orleans. Also she preferred New Orleans, she felt more at ease there. She could if she wanted to walk around the whole of it in a day, not LA as it was much bigger with a much bigger divide between the rich and poor.

Monday lunch time she drove over the river into New Orleans near City Park. Stopped in the parks carpark and got out and stretcher, if you were blind you would still know you were in New Orleans by its smell and sound she thought. Even Maggie as she sat on the seat next to her knew before they even got near the bridge to cross into New Orleans, she moved to the front of the RV. There was something about the place, it got under your skin. As soon as she'd parked up near her place and started getting her dirty clothes in a pillowcase and left over food in a brown paper bag, Collected the last couple of tin's of tuna that were for her cat. And walked to her place, where she put the clothes in the machine and the food on the kitchen counter as she was dying for a good long soak in the bath as she felt dirty for some reason.

After the bath she made coffee and put the pastry's she'd bought on her journey there on a plate and settled herself in front of her Laptop as she needed to find out all she could about identity disorder also if there could be any other reason to memory loose. As she just could not believe the alternative as that frightened her.

After several hours she found no illness linked with Memory loose other than a tumour or a hit on the head, neither she had. Summer got up and walked into the bedroom and stood in front of the tall mirror and called out to her other self to reveal her self. But of course nothing happened. She'd read on line that some people have more than 2 at least she only had one other.

Maggie had come into the sitting room to ask for food, yes Maggie looking at the time, she'd been at it hours and it was gone 7pm I'm hungry as well. So decided to feed her then pop out to the Cafe on the corner and buy a take away as she decided to look up her parents on line, as her stepfather had a lot to answer for, as this was down to him.

Back from the Cafe and once again sitting in front of the Laptop she told it, I'm going to look you up on line to see if you're still the Mayor of Seattle or if you are still even living there. I'v not bother to look you up since I left so here goes nothing she said aloud.

She'd been sitting in the dark in front of a blank screen for a couple of hours just staring at it. Outside it was dark as she just sat there, a shocked look on her face. Maggie had walked back and forth in front of her on top of the Laptop, something she normally would be mad at her for and put her down on the floor, but not this time.

Suddenly she pulled herself together. What she'd read on line about her stepfather she just couldn't believe as it wasn't possible no way?

As Maggie went to walk over the Laptop again, pulled her off and held her close to her chest before talking to her. Maggie it's not possible my stepfather is dead. Been dead since the night I left home. Did you know that all this time I have been wanted for murdering him that night. There was a poster of me on line and an award if anyone knew my were about? It was hard to take it all in after all this time. I should feel something by the news. It was just a shock finding out after all this time. Thats something I can't blame my other self for as I remember every minutes of that night, although I didn't intend to kill him as I didn't wish him dead just to leave me alone.

Oh well nothing I can do about it now, I'm not turning myself in. It's been nearly four since it happened, I expect they have had more murders since then even worse one, in any case he was a rotten Mayor. And I don't look much like my photo on screen after so long. Kissed Maggie and put her down on the floor closed the Laptop and got up and went over and put the TV on and sat on the couch and relaxed as the early evening news was about to finish, so she only caught the end of it before the weather forecast. Picked her cell phone up and Phoned Jason to let him know she was back.

Jason was glad to hear from her as he'd missed her lots, and told her that and invited her to lunch the next day at his place. She could tell him all her news then as it was late and he was busy. Love you babe see you at noon sleep well?

You as well Jason, and I missed you as well.

I'm surprised to hear that but glad you did babe, sorry I have to go we have a large group of rowdy guys in who won't leave. Bye babe?

Bye Jason, put the phone down and decided to have an early night.

Next morning she woke with a headache and knew straight away that she'd been out Clubbing or what ever her other half did.

God I wish I knew why this is happening to me. Got out of bed only to find the clothes her other self had warn were strewn over the floor, her purse was on her chair. Opened it hoping to find were she had been. There were casino chips in side the purse, quite a good amount. Counted it and found at least several hundred dollars in chips.

Maybe if she went to the Casino to cash them in, someone there might know how she came by them, because as far as she knew she didn't gamble.

Maggie came out of the spare room where she'd sleep last night as her mistress was out.

Shame you can't talk Maggie as you could tell me what my other self is like? I'll get your food before I shower putting on the coffee and TV news before she fed her.

Left the clothes on the floor, you inside me can pick your own dirty clothes up as I'm not your slave, banging the bathroom door behind her as she was pissed off and mad by it all. It was the not remembering she hated as she cursed, as she climb in under the hot shower to calm down.

After getting dressed she decided to go shopping for food and more headache pills, then after dropping them back she was off to the casino before lunch with Jason. She'd decided not to tell him anything about her other identity. And had decided to give her a name, Lilith the first wife of Adam who left the Garden of Eden and became the mother of demons as I feel you are my demon she said a loud hoping Lilith could hear her. Mother always said that my Sunday bible read at morning services would come in handy.

Standing outside the Casino after taking the Street car there she had know Idea how she was going to broach the subject of last night once in side to any one? Took a deep breath and walked on in. Even on a Tuesday it was full of locals gambling on the fruit machines. She looked around to see where she could cash in her chips, when a man dressed in a dark suit and tie and white shirt walked over to her

You're back early Miss, introducing him self as Roger the floor manager. You're not on till tonight. The patrons here really love your voice. Last night was a joy to here you again. So what can I do for you?

Came back to cash in my chips so if you could point me in the right direction to cash them in please?

Ye's of course Miss, Roger replied it seemed you were lucky last night playing Black Jack with such little stake money.

She couldn't remember any of it, but at least she could fill in the blanks in her memory. And at least Lilith didn't do anything bad thank god.

There is one thing you can tell me, what time I'm playing tonight as I have forgotten?

Nine to night in the club bar, I'll stay late so I can hear you. Last evening when you were asked by the Club manager if you would sing for the patrons and tonight as well as he remembered you singing there before. And you agreed, I was surprise that you said yes as your band is in LA still I believe.

Summer smiled and told Roger that she was at her happiest when singing. Then left him to see to a big fat lady who had just hit the jackpot on the fruit machine, and it was spitting out coins all over the floor in front of it.

At the cashier desk the woman there counted out 7 hundred and 47 dollar's in notes to her. Are you sure you wouldn't rather have a cashier cheque Miss, as it's a lot to be carrying around with you?

No thanks, I'll be fine but thanks any way stuffing the money in her bag. If any one saw her there, she'd use her skills as a kick boxing, As she was amateur ladies champion in Louisiana last year. After over three years she was good at it, and it had built up a muscular body as well as muscles on her arms as well so she wasn't worried about carrying such a large sum on herself.

Suddenly she remembered her luncheon date with Jason, she'd forgotten all about it after all that had happened. She'd be late rushing out to see if there was a taxi any where near rather than wait around for the streetcar as the taxi would take her straight to the door. Luckily one pulled up out side to deposit a couple for the Casino. So she asked the driver if he was free now to take her to The Balcony Restaurant and Guest house and club.

Ye's Miss please get in?

She was so relieved that he would take her over the other side of New Orleans. As not all taxi companies go in to Marigny around frenchman and that end of Royal. And sat back to enjoy the ride although it would cost she expected around 40 or so dollars, the streetcar would have only cost her 3 dollars with a walk of a few hundred yards the rest of the way. But she did have a bundle of notes in her purse so this time it was worth it.

Summer got out and paid the drive 50 dollars from her bundle. Then walked over to the restaurant door and couldn't see Jason inside. She was over an hour late so couldn't blame him as she walked along to the open bar door and looked through, and there was Jason talking to some customers. She took a deep breath and went inside and walked over to him, ready to say sorry and to make it up to him she'd tell him she'd sing for free Wednesday evening. After he'd finished talking to the customers she said just that. And waited for him to reply?

He stood looking at her his hands on his hips. You better have a good reason for ruining a good meal?

I had private business Jason, and forgot the time. I'm here now and I'm sure the meal can be microwaved, I do it all the time. Thats what they are for and you have a big industrial one in the kitchen Jason.

That is not the point Summer? And you can go and ask chief to do just that as I'm not. I need him to work tonight, not walk out at the mention of reheating his food.

Okay I'll go and ask him nicely Jason, walking through the adjoining door into the Restaurant followed by Jason.

All went well meal wise, it tasted nice she thought and the chilled wine was very nice as she sat after the meal sipping it. Don't know what all the fuss was about with the chief Jason?

Jason smiled and sipped his cold beer. I miss you when you go so far away babe. Will you be spending the night with me here like last week?

Have a gig at the Casino club room and I expect it to be late like last night so cain't sorry.
I'll stay tomorrow night after I'v sung for my meal.

Very funny babe, but you dropped by last night after 1 till gone 4 am, when you said you had to get back for your cat for some reason. I wanted to wake up with you naked beside me in the morning. But I'm happy to have even a couple of hours with you babe, I love you so much. And I'm sure you feel the same way after the way you made love to me, boy was it passionate.

After hearing all he had to say she took a big gulp of wine and poured out another glass and drank it down in one. As all this wasn't known to her. So Lilith had taken their relationship further like I now believe in the RV in LA. She had an Idea that she had lost her virginity way back but couldn't be sure till now. Shame she couldn't remember any of it as sex was supposed to be enjoyable, as she sat silent not knowing how to answer.

Jason asked if she was okay, you didn't regret there sexual relationship as he put his arm around her and kissed her neck fondly.

Summer felt aroused by it as he kissed her behind her ear then ran his fingers down her back.
If you have know where else to be yet maybe you and I could go and make love up stairs in my room. I can repay you by making love to you like you did me by going down on you before entering you.

She hadn't the slyest intention of making love to him when she arrived and walked into the bar that lunchtime to see him, only after all that sexual talk and touching from him she was now, and kissed him on the lips passionately. Up stairs they quickly tore each others clothes off and left them where they fell as he picked her naked body up in his arms her legs intwined around his naked waist as he walked over to the bed and dropped her down on it, and fell on top of her kissing her passionately on the lips then her neck and took her small breast in each hand and sucked each one.

Summer was in heaven her whole body was a live, something she'd never felt only Lilith her other self. As Jason's tongue licked her body as it went down her body till he got to her shaven pussy. Lifted up her legs opening them and eat her pussy till she squealed with pleasure, he then entered her with his firm thick cock and brought them both to a climax. Summer lay in his arms as they both to stock of what had just happened between them.

Summer because this was her first, and Jason because he never wanted it to end but go on for every as his wife, and lay there wondering how he'd ask her.

Babe that was wonderful, I'v only bee'n with you a couple of times. Each time it gets better. You as a person get better around me. We have gone from good friends to lovers in just over 3 years, and have been through a lot together. Tomorrow I'm coming with you to see the Therapist. You helped me though my mothers accidentally death, I don't know how I'd coped if it hadn't been for you. I want you to marry me. Want to take care of you like you do me. I love you so much Summer, so what do you say babe?

Summer had listened in silence and so wanted to say yes, but how could she with Lilith in her head. Know way could she till she'd got rid of her if that were possible?

Jason until I get my memory loose cured. Which will mean a lot of therapy, so I can't yet much as I'd like to, so please understand if I ask you to wait?

I can wait babe as long as I know you will be mine when you're better.

What if I don't Jason, what then, as I can't ask you to keep waiting?

I'v got to believe you will babe, and with that he made love with her all over again.

Back at her place she felt alive after all that loving. Stood looked in the mirror and spoke to her other self. You're not going to have it all your own way with my body anymore as she started getting ready for the gig at the casino. She knew she'd never be able to live a normal life let alone marry Jason not with the other identity inside her head. She was fooling herself that tomorrows therapist with be able to help her. Looked in the mirror at her self in a short sleeved V necked short blue fitted dress, her hair up in a roll and a beautiful clip and told herself in the mirror that she liked what she saw, if it wern't for you Lilith I could be happy.

Tonight Lilith after the gig I'm going back to Jason and stay with him for a few hours, are you listening Lilith. I'm going to stay awake for as long as I can so you can't take me over, do you hear as she shouted loudly at the mirror. Maggie was hiding in the second bedroom under the bed as she'd never heard her mistress shout angrily at herself before.

Outside the taxi had just pulled up to take her to the Casino. Summer looked around for Maggie to hug her before leaving and couldn't find her at first, till saw Maggie's eyes shining under the bed from the hall light. And bent and spoke softly to her until she came out from under it. Sorry if I scared you babe girl hugging her, neither of us will ever hurt you baby. Theirs a dish of fresh cooked fish from Jason's on the kitchen counter for you with fresh cat's milk beside it in a dish I'll be gone till dawn babe kissing her then put her on the couch picked up her bag and left.

CHAPTER 8

The gig at the Casino went well, and she agreed to do it twice a week solo, with just her playing the piano. The money would come in handy she told Marshall "the new CEO of the Casino" as herself and the boys were launching a new DVD of her new songs in an LA music studio. Cost a fair bit, and they were due to start when she got back there. The guys had arranged it all behind her back while she was away here last time. She didn't even know how much for some reason as the guys didn't want to bother her with any of the details. And she'd had enough on her plate to bother to ask them.

Marshall after the gig offered to pay for her to do a solo DVD at the local music studio here, to sell in his place at first. Split the money 50-50.

Summer liked the Idea and agreed. And they toasted their new adventure. She liked Marshall as you knew where you stood with him unlike the last CEO there who was murdered.

Okay I'll set it up for next week Wednesday morning around 9 30. Okay with you?

Sounds fine Marshall, only I'll need a decent secondhand portable Electric piano from some where to use in stead of that old piano that I believe the studio here has.

Okay i'll try and get you a decent one for your personal use.

During the ride that night in the taxi to Jason from the Casino she went though all that Marshall had said, and Jason. If she gave up the gigs in LA with the boys. She was sure they'd find a singer to replace her or use Bryan like before she joined. Then she could spend more time on her own singing career and her relationship with Jason. And as she was going to have her first session with the therapy's to morrow, it would be better she we're here rather than there full time for now. And now she was going to have her own CDS and a video as well it made sence.

The taxi pulled up out side Jasons Club as she was still deep in thought. A voice said we are here Miss. Bringing her from her thoughts, thanked him and gave him a tip and got out on a high, as she'd made up her mind what she was going to do.

The Club was still packed altho it was pass 1pm. Jason was pleased to see her and stoped what he was doing behind the bar and came over and hugged and kissed her. How was the gig babe looking at her dress, you look beautiful babe should wear a dress more often?

She smiled and asked if she could have a coffee? My throats a bit dry.

Come babe sit I'll get you your coffee.

We'll be closing soon. We had a young crowd all evening, not so rowdy tonight. How was your crowd as I expect they are more mature and from business sector?

Customers were business men some with their wives or girlfriends. There to listen to me over a good meal and wine. I have more gigs there solo and one at a banquet in the Capitol at their town hall not bad money either, and I don't have to share it. Don't look at me like that, I know I should let the guys know but this is for me not them. And I am to make a CD and video paid for by Marshall. We share 50/50 no strings attached on sales. And they will be sold at my gigs and in the Casino shop. What do you think?

Does that mean you're thinking of giving up Los Angeles gigs babe?

Ye's Jason, I need to be near my therapist so I can go twice a week. The new gigs mean I can do that as I wasn't happy in LA. I had a lot more memory loose there. And it scares me as I have any Idea what I do at night.

Like sleeping that first night with me babe. I realised yesterday that you had know memory of our first sexual encounter, but didn't say anything.

And I'm sure you don't do anything bad, you're to nice a person. So you going to tell the guys at the weekend, they won't be happy you do realise.

I know but it's my life, and they can manage without me as Bryan sings, and they we're on there own long before I joined them. And at first it was meant to be temporally. I'll do the gigs next weekend but that will be it.

I'll come with you just incase they get nasty babe. As you're not under contract with them.

Summer quickly said no, I'll be fine Jason. I'd rather handle them alone. You being there might make things worse but thanks. I'll phone you often to keep in touch.

If you think it best babe, but phone me straight after you have told them. And promise me that you will straight away come home here and leave them to it. As you say they sang okay before you?

I promise Jason. Now I'll help you lock up as it looks like the place is emptying. Then bed yes?

It was Wednesday morning and they were both off to the therapist. Altho Jason wouldn't be going in with her, but wait in reception. Summer was glad to have him beside her in stead of facing it on her own. Whether she could be honest with him after. And tell him what she was told by the therapist she wasn't sure?

In the business centre of New Orleans was were the Clinic was situated among the small collection of sky scrapers that New Orleans had. They parked out in front as there were no underground car parks because of the boggy soil in New

Orleans. Summer was nerves and wondered if her other self knew what was happening?

Jason took her hand and led her up to the clinic doors and inside to reception. She stood they, as she couldn't get the words out so Jason gave her name to the receptionist letting go of her hand and put it around her waist. The receptionist said the doctor want keep them waiting, only she still had a patient with her. So Jason led her to a line of seats along a wall. Babe you have know reason to be nerves. I'm sure she will find and find a simple reason why you have hours of memory loose. Their has to be a simple expiration for it, trying to make her feel better.

But she didn't, as she knew dissociative identity disorder was not a normal illness to be cured with a pill, and you couldn't cut out that part of the brain to cure her. Her hands were sweaty as she sat there.

Then a door opened and a young man came out, behind him Summers doctor. They walked up to reception and the doctor made him another appointment and told him to keep up with his medication. So he has something medication can help, so some mental illness can be cured with pill's which made her feel a little better.

On seeing her the doctor came up and welcomed her and accompanied to her room.

How are you feeling Miss Dala-Rosa, have you had any more memory looses pointing to the couch please sit? The Neurologists passed your details to me as I have a certificate so I can legally Hypnotise you if necessary.

Summer sat tongue tied for a couple of minutes. Then told herself not to be silly the doctor was there to help her. And begun by telling her all that had happened while she was in Los Angeles.

I also just found out that I had started sleeping with my boyfriend, when I had no recollection of it Dr

Novikou? I thought I was still a virgin, altho I had a feeling inside of me that I wasn't. Can you help me as I feel as if I am going mad. And my memory loose is lasting longer. And I ran away from home at 17 to here.

Tell me when did you first notice it happening as she turned on a recording machine to record their section's.

When I first got to New Orleans, and only at night?

Do you know of anything that might have trigged it off, you say you ran away from home? As she looked at her notes on her computer.

Summer told her about her stepfather leaving out the bit where she kills him.

You say you were assaulted by your stepfather while your mother was out?

My stepfather started doing it when I was eleven years, when they got married, whenever we were along. When I started my period he'd go up the back way making me bleed and it always hurt.

Did you tell your mother?

Not till I was in my teens, as I was scared of him while I was little as he'd scare me from telling any one.

And that last time did something different happen between you for you to leave home and move a cross country?

Ye's I had enough and was ready for him. So when he came into my room in a dressing gown naked underneath it. And came over to me thinking I would allow him to have his way. As he'd got more adventure's in his sexual advances which I hated. I hit him. for the first time and fought him off.

Then I left, so don't know how he is now. As it's been a few years now. "that was not quite true but she was not a bout to tell the doctor".

That could have triggered it, as it must have been traumatic for you. And as you say you had already decided not to put up with it any more so your mind was always on the alert never at peace.

Maybe if you went back home and confronted him now you're older and have a career, I saw you sing last evening at the casino. Maybe this would put your mind at rest and stop the memory loss, do you think you could do that with your boyfriend?

She knew this was impossible now, as he was dead. And she couldn't think of a good reason to tell the doctor why she couldn't. May I ask you something doctor is what I tell you here in you office stay in your office, what I mean is it private?

The doctor replied that she was like a priest in the confessional. So what ever she said would stay with her.

You will have to turn of your tape record also Doctor, other wise I can't tell you?

If you wish Miss, reaching over and turning it off. Now Miss what is it that you have to say that I can't record or that I can't mention?

My stepfather was Major of Seattle, and it seemed he was we'll liked by people. So when I got into my teens and he still raped me, he'd say afterwards that if I did tell, who would believe me as I was a no body, not even of his flesh. I did look him up not long ago on line. It seemed I hurt him and he reported me to the police. So you see I can't go back ever, which means I'm stuck with this?

The doctor took her time in answering, then replied, if what you say about your stepfather and why you attacked him I would have thought the police would treat it as self defence surly?

I can't take that chance sorry. You don't know my mother. She never believed me and put it down to being jealous of her time with him, as my real father dumped my mother when he knew she was with child. She told me that she was only his girl friend and she did not realise she was pregnant for a while. Her mother said she would help her to look after me if she kept it. My mother made sure I knew all that just before she married the monster.

I'm so sorry Miss. So it leave only one thing I can do, and that is to find out what you are like when you change and loose your memory. "Hypnotise you". Until I have seen both sides of the problem I can't work out the best treatment. So what do you say?

If you think it will help you to treat me, of course yes? I'm away from tomorrow will be back Monday late. So any day after that I can come as I'm not going back to LA till I'm my self again. Then only on my terms as a solo artist.

Okay then let me look at my appointments for next week and see where I can fit you in, as I'd like to see you twice a week from now on if that is okay with you?

That's sounds okay thank you doctor.

Then let me check and see what day and time, going on her Computer and after a few minutes gave her two appointments. There is one thing Miss, does your boyfriend know about your dissociative Identity disorder as I feel it would help you if he did. And might help towards curbing you as time goes on?

Jasons doesn't know and until I know if I can be cured. Would rather he didn't. As I believe my Lilith my other character is violent after finding bloody clothes hidden a year back. Then I didn't know about split personality, and put the clothes out of my mind.

You gave her a name? Not a good Idea as it makes it more difficult to treat you. I would stop using it from now on Miss. Write down every time it happens and what you were doing just before and just after when you wake from your memory loose. Even what you were wearing before and after you loose your memory. Right see you next Tuesday afternoon, she got up and went out to reception with Summer to greet her next patient.

Jason got up and greeted her. How did go babe?

I'm going to be hypnotise to see what I am like when my memory goes. Also keep a written diary of the before and after which I did do some times. Next Tuesday afternoon is when it will happen. Now Jason can you drop me along the Riverwalk as I need to think and get some fresh air as well. Why is it clinics spell of hospital disinfectant? I hate the smell.

Babe I'll walk with you and then we can have lunch some where nice later in the French quarter, what do you say? I'll also make sure I'm free to come to your appointments so you don't have to go through all this on your own?

I need to be along right now to think, so if you don't mind just dropping me off, you could come back after an hour or so and we can have lunch that would be great. Also the appointments, I'd love you to be with me.

Sitting outside the Sea Aquarium on riverwalk she wondered if her other identity new what the doctor was saying. She had know Idea what the thing in her head was capable of. What she had read about split personality, was that it's like a double sided cone. The gentle caring side and the more out going side, not an actual other person. That was most likely why the doctor told her to drop calling it by a name.

I wonder what Jame would say if I told him? If someone I loved told me I don't know how Idea feel. Why oh why does life have to be so complicated. My stepfather has a lot to answer for if he were a live. She suddenly burst into tears and put her head in her lap and sobbed.

A hand went on her back and a soft voice asked if she was okay. Lifting her head she saw it was the priest from the St Louis Cathedral in Jackson Square. He was holding the biggest Po'boy that was dripping with meat, veg and sauce.

Do you mind if I sit beside you he asked her, oh about my roll, I have to sneak away to get one and eat it in secret as my housekeeper would scold me for eating it. She has me on a health kick touching his slightly big stomach?

Hearing him talk suddenly calmed her for some reason. She replied that she was glad to have his company right now.

He introduced himself as Father Mathew, and would she like half of his roll?
Thankyou but no as I'm going out to lunch with my boyfriend later. My names Summer Dalla-Rosa.

May I ask why you were sobbing earlier,
It can't be so bad surely child? It sometimes help to talk about what's worrying you to a complete stranger?

Summer so wanted to unload herself, and a priest might even help her right now. What is on my mind is not easy to talk about to anyone, and it could also lead to me getting into trouble so as much as I wish I could just tell someone I can't?

Are you a Catholic child or a christian, as you could tell me in my confessional and I would have to keep it to myself or be disrobed so you can tell me anything child?

For once she suddenly felt relieved to be able to unburden herself after so long, yes she would so like to unburden herself to him.
Okay Miss but first let me finish this before walking back to my Church.

After what seemed like hours she'd told him everything from the age of eleven till present day. Leaving nothing out, even waking up to bruises and a bloody dress, her flick knife with dried blood on it and even her stepfather being dead and she did it. And what she had found out about split identity on line, even what the doctor had said.

She got up to walk out of the confessional box when Father Mathew told her to stay put as he has to reply to her inside the confessional for it to be bond by holy orders. So she sat back down.

He surprised her by believing that all people have two sides to their nature, one more defined than the other. You and your stepfather coming to a head brought out the dormant side of you. So when you are confronted by someone who might caused you harm or stress the dormant side takes over. So you don't have to face your emulsion's.

I have dealt with this before at my first church in New Mexico a young lad who saw his mother brutally murdered in front of him when he was 9 years. He had been a quiet polite boy up till then, afterwards he became a thug. Only his quiet side knew nothing of this.

So did he get cured, and if so how father?

I'm afraid he went to far one day in his other state and killed someone and is now in prison. His violent side has completely gone now he is in there, he's 14 now doing 5 years. We were having bible lesson and prayer's up till that fateful day, and we were making good progress but for that one event which he didn't start. Which the judge took into account so didn't treat it as murder just manslaughter? I visit him when I can. So you see you're not the only one, there are others out there like you.

Summer listened with deep interest, then asked father Mathew do you think bible reading and praying might help me, as I am at my wits end? I can't make plan's that might cause my other side to show. My boyfriend wants to marry me but how can I? My boyfriend, oh my god I'm supposed to meet him on riverwalk by Cafe du-Monde looking at her watch it had been over 2 hours he'll be worried sick thinking I might have killed my self or run away what ever? I have to phone him let him know where I am stepping out of the confessional, her legs were a little stiff as she did so.

Before you phone him Summer I'd like to try and help you, It was to late for that young lad but not for you, so please let me try with Gods help?

Summer thanked him and said she'd like that very much, so when can we start?

How about after evening service tonight, you could come too as it can't hurt, so what do you say?

I have a gig at 9 so what time is service father?

It starts at 7 and finishes at 7:45 so you could start straight after till 8:35 pm. If you order a taxi before hand and get the drive to be outside here at that time you will just make your gig without any stress, what do you think?

I'll be in church father at 7 and I'll wear my grandmother silver amethyst cross from now on. I did wear it when I was younger.

You do realise one thing miss, you have to have faith and believe in God for it to work, and keep believing. That is the most important thing?

I use to go to church as a child with my mother right up till I left home. But I couldn't believe that if there was a God why did he let my stepfather continue to rape me? So I stopped when I left home.

God can't stop people doing bad things, but he can help to heal the wound after my child. And that is what I will try to do in his name. So I'll see you this evening and from now on every evening till hopefully you are back to your old self. Then if you come to church on a Sunday and easter, Christmas so on then I'm sure you will be happy once more with Gods blessing.

Summer knelt in front of the cross and crossed herself and said a few words. Then got up and switched her phone on as she'd turned it off in the church. Jason had tried to get through several times. She phoned him once outside the box, and as soon as she heard his voice before he could speak she blurted out where she was and she'd wait there for him outside by the jazz band that was playing then turned it off before he could reply. Bowed to wards the Alter and walked out into the afternoon air feeling a lot better in herself as she did believed in God, and at least she was trying something herself besides the doctor.

The music was a pleasant distraction from her problems, as she put money in the bands box. And sat on a seat in the square. There was no where like it in the world and she loved the place, it got under your skin and you couldn't shake it off if you wanted to. Where else was there art work of all kinds hang on the wrought iron fences surrounding the square and always at least a couple of bands playing different music trying to out do the other and attract tourist to buy the CD's or put money in their box's. And the different smells from different restaurants surrounding the area. She knew she didn't want to live anywhere else no matter what happens. Just then a very frantic looking Jason came rushing up to her.

Thank God you'r safe I was so worried after your section at the doctors. You are okay yes?

I wasn't but after an elderly Priest caught me crying and took me under his wing I feel less stressed and frightened.

I'm going to church tonight at 7 then stay behind for bible reading class's. It might help my head as I have to do something. And I can't seeing me being hypnotise can help me. The doc will just go over my lost hours and see me as I am when I loose my memory. It won't stop it happening again.

There is no magic pill I can take. I don't want to talk about it any more, I'm hungry so let's find some where I can get my teeth into the food, not slouch okay.

Jason knew there was no point in trying to talk to her about what just happened, he'd just have to wait for her to trust him enough to tell him what's going on. He could wait as he loved her so much, and would die for her if necessary, Okay babe where do you want to eat as it's way gone lunch time?

Summer replied I fancy Jambalaya with lots of different sea food and ham and meat at Sobou Restaurant, here in the French Quarter. It stay's open till 11 tonight so what do you say?

At least we can walk to it from here as my feet are killing me after trying to find you babe, he then took hold of her hand, and they walked towards the area where Sobou's restaurant was.

The time at the church with the father was pleasant for her. Jason would have liked to have come next time but had trade's people coming at his business's. Summer was glad as she didn't want him to know anything about her past, till she had no more memory looses.

That first session with father Mathew made her feel at easy a little with her memory loose mood swings. And after every session she felt a little better and had, had no memory lose. She'd changed before going to the church so was already for her gig which also always went well. She even told one of the proprietor that she was free to do a couple of early ones over the week end. As she'd made a decision to tell the guys she won't be coming that weekend as she had doctors appointment and other appointments as well that she couldn't get out of. How they'd take it she had know Idea.

Summer decided to take the streetcar as far as it would take her to her area and home. And sat sending email's to Bryan and Paul before she chicken out now she'd made up her mind to go every evening to the church for a section with the father. She didn't want to take the risk of getting stressed out by their reaction when she told them she wasn't leaving New Orleans face to face, and then loose her memory and do something stupid in LA.

Jason wouldn't pleased she was taking the street car so late. Only taxi's we're expensive 40 dollars when for 3 dollars she could get within three quarters of a mile home. He would have offer to pay for the taxi to keep her safe but no, 40 dollars verses 3 dollars would have been criminal when some people in the world are starving so she'd not told Jason.

And in any case it was cooler at night, more local people were about because it was. Only tourist were about in forty degree humid heat during the day unless locals had business.

Half way home on the Streetcar she started feeling dizzy, and stopped to get her head together. A man a local from down the street asked her for a cigarette as he was out?

Sorry I don't smoke and quickly moved on to another seat away from him, as she had a feeling she'd been a position like this before but couldn't remember the details.

You live a short distant away from my place the man replied moving nearer, then it was her stop as the streetcar pulled up. She got up and got off knowing he'd follow her. Which he did and caught up with her.

Summer turned and looked at him. He'd had a lot to drink, as he smelt of it. Also he was shabby dressed, and she had evening wear on and heels. Not that it bothered her he was shabby. It was his manner that bothered her as he lend towards her holding a half empty Rum bottle. Have a drink girly make you more pleasant as you seem up tight?

Summer ignore him and quickly walked on out of his reach, then began to run till she got to her place, and ran up the steps to her door. Thumbled around in her bag for her door key and quickly opened it, rushed inside just in time as he'd reached her gate.

She closed and double locked the door and leaned against it relieved she had made it as she had a funny Idea he wanted something more than a cigarette. Turned on the lamp near her, kicked off her shoes and walked into the kitchen and put on a pot of coffee, bent and picked up Maggie and held her close. I expect your hungry old lady? And put her down on the counter and got Maggie some fish before getting herself a blueberry muffin from the cake tin, poured out a coffee and took them into her bedroom and put some music on, then took of her dress dropping it on the floor and sat on the bed put her feet up and relaxed.

It had been an interesting eventful day and now she was tired. And just wanted to forget for a while. Before her email was read by the boys, then there angry replied most likely will have a lot of swear words in it. She was glad she'd decided not to tell them in person, taking a bite out of the muffin as Maggie jumped up on top of her and curled up and purred.

Thursday morning came around too quick as Maggie walked over her face purring. Summer reached for the clock, it said 7. For god sake Maggie can't a person have a lye in turning over. Maggie was having nothing of it, she was hungry and she was her provider of her food so she sat on top of her still purring.

Okay girl I'm up see, as she got up out of bed stretched her body and walked to the kitchen to open a tin of cat food before showering.

As she sat out on the veranda with her breakfast, the heat hadn't set in jet so she would take the opportunity to sit out on her veranda almost her colourful flowering pot plants and climbing sweet smelling rose that had started to twined it self around the post of her veranda and along the top. Why would anyone want to live any where else she thought as she sipped her fresh coffee?

Just then her neighbour next door came out side, seeing her he asked shouldn't you be on your way to Sin City? The wife was going to check on your place as usual while you'r away?

Summer laughter, why do you call it that I don't know? I'm not going to Los Angeles any more unless I get a one night stand at a big Club or Concert Hall to drag me all the way there. Only made up my mind yesterday not to go. Thank your miss's for me.

Glad to hear you'r not going every weekend. Place not the same without you singing through the walls of your place in to the street. It sounds so sweet even the birds stop sing to listen.

Mr Robinson you exaggerate.

Have to say au revisor, as off to work miss. As he got into his car he called out to her, we'll have one of our late night street parties at the weekend and as you'r not leaving would you sing for us?

I'd like that, and I will be able to play music as well with you two. As I will have a digital keyboard I can carry around with me to gigs and plug it in.

Even better miss, we can join in with you and make the street swing and bring the surrounding neighbourhood out, must go speak to you later.

Summer stroked Maggie who was sitting on a seat beside her. Maybe one day I'll earn enough to buy this place like the rest of the street, what do you say. Just then her phone went it was Bryan in LA.

Here goes nothing picking up her phone off the table beside her, and said hi then put it to speaker to listen. After a few minutes she switched it off saying nothing in reply. There was no point as they were so mad with her, and threatened all sought's of thing's that they'd do to her, even sue her for breach of contract. Which she knew they couldn't as there was no contract and there was no point in talking to them either? They did have one good point, she was letting them down at short notice but couldn't help it.

There was a text from Jason as well on the phone, he'd expected her to stay overs his place last night and wondered why she hadn't?

All she wanted to do was get her head clear and get some more gigs to replace LA's. She didn't want to be tied down she realised yet to marriage, not until she was well established in the Music business. And now with her new CD she was going to make Friday instead of next week, as she'd told the CEO Marshall at the Casino before her gig there last evening about LA which he was glad about.

After a good week so far with no memory loose, The CD went well, and she was pleased when she heard her voice. The visits to Father at the church she felt were helping, now was her visit one to Dr Novikov to be Hypnotise in the morning. And she was terrified of what might happen. She even thought about not going as she had the Father helping her. Jason had talked her into going and was going to pick her up in a few minutes out side the Casino to spend the night with him so she didn't have to spend a sleepless night worrying about it. Standing there in the cooler night air after being 40 degrees that day,

She had news to tell him. She had a gig in Baton Rouge on Saturday evening at the state capital's Ball. Then the following weekend at Grand Isle golf club charity dinner advent, and she could do both in two hour's and back. Also she can bring someone to the Charity advent dinner for victims of flooding in Florida who lost everything, so she'd ask Jason.

She was to sing and help to auction the goods business's had donated including Marshall, who put forward her name to sing and help out as well. And she'd get a first class meal there as well.

Marshall had got both gigs for her so she'd stay in the area, he'd told her after her last gig. As he was hoping she'd meant it when she mentioned a week earlier that she was not happy with going to LA and was thinking of pulling out. He'd hoped the gigs would show her she could have a great career without them and he wasn't taking out any money from them either. It had been a gamble incase she turned the new gigs down, because she felt she couldn't let LA guys down, but it paid off.

All this was going through her head as well as tomorrows visit to the doctor as she stood outside the well lite Casino waiting for Jason to pull up.

The next morning sitting out on the balcony of Jason's guest house sipping coffee and eating a blueberry muffin for breakfast with Jason sitting next to her eating a stuffed bacon roll with spicy brown sauce that was dripping on to the ground as he held it. She didn't know how he could eat it so early in the morning as she couldn't.

I could get use to this smiling at her as he took a big bite of the roll.

You could, could you, Your waist line would disappear below your belt before long she replied?

Very funny babe, you know very well I mean you being here with me for breakfast after a passionate night of love.

Summer smiled but said nothing, then after finishing her Muffin she replied that she had to get back to her place to feed Maggie and change in to casual wear, you coming with me or will you meet me outside the doctor's at 11 as it's 9 now?

I'll take you back to your place and wait. Then we can go together to the doctor's. You should have brought a change of clothing with you last evening?

She told him firmly that she'd still have Maggie to feed, can't neglect my cat now can I?

That bloody cat, I'm sure you think more about it than any one else including me?

Summer ignored his words, got up and walked inside and down the stairs to the street. And started walking back to her place, she was upset by his words as she didn't think he had a nasty bone in his body "She was now wrong".

Jason got into his car and caught up to her, slowly drove along side of her with the window down. Sorry babe it just came out about your cat. I didn't mean it honestly, please get in the car?

Summer stoped and turned to him, it's just a defenceless cat that I love, and take my responsibility for looking after it seriously, getting in beside him.

The heat and humidity was beating down on both of them as they stood outside the clinic, as she stood hesitant to go inside. The thought of being hypnotises and not being able to be in charge of her own answers to the doctors question's as she is under, scares her.

Jason put his hand on her arm, it's all right to be scared babe, as I think I would. But if you want her to help you, you have to know what triggers your memory loose when you lose your memory. It makes sence babe, because if you know what triggers it then maybe you can stop it happening when you see the sign's.

Summer knew he was right, and slowly started walking towards the clinic doors then inside and stood silent at the reception.

Jason took charge and gave Summers name and the doctor she had an appointment to see. Dr Novikov is waiting, as you're late. James said sorry the traffic was bad, not true but he wasn't going to say that they had words and Summer had stormed off, so that was why.

The doctor was told that they were there and came out of her office. Summer was holding Jasons hand tightly as the doctor greeted them and escorted her, and to her surprise Jason to her office. Once inside the doctor asked if it was appropriate that he should be with them while she was hypnotise? Summer nodded yes and sat down on the couch, Jason sat down a little distance from her on it.

Not what the doctor wanted, as she wanted her lying on it not sitting as it works better lying down but said nothing, as this would be her first case of identity disorder. Not that she was going to tell her that.

Now please sit comfortable and relax and look straight a head, as she held a small silver ball with a light at it's centre front of her face, that started to rotate, slow at first then faster and faster as she stared into it. You are feeling sleepy so close your eyes. Now concentrate back to your first memory loose. You have just finished your gig and are walking back to your place.

Summer sat on the couch clutching hold of Jasons hands tightly, her eyes were sore from the light in her face rotating fast and she didn't feel sleepy at all, and waited for something to happen but no nothing. She could hear the doctors voice clearly and feel the warmth of Jasons hand in hers but nothing else.

The doctor then asking her to go back to before she left home. That faithful night that started it all, as she wasn't getting anywhere asking about her first memory loose was, but nothing as she sat silent?

In the end she opened her eyes and shouted get that bloody light from my face, as that light hurt's my eyes as she'd waited to go under hypnotic. It's not working doc, nothing except my sore eyes sorry?

Disappointed as it was a waste of her time. She told her not every one can be hypnotised and it seems you're one of them. I'm afraid I can't help you, as there is no way of me knowing what the trigger is, and without that information I can't treat you I'm am so sorry. With those words she got up to show them out. Then she had a thought, maybe it was because you having your young man so close to you, and I noticed you holding hands could be the reason. We could try again on your next appointment alone, what do you say?

Summer looked at her with a weird look on her face, I'll think about it and ring you and let you know before you cancel my other appointments, turned and walked out of the room still holding Jasons hand her eyes red and sore.

All that time he'd not said anything, as they walked through reception and straight outside without her even paying for the session. They both then got in the car, and Jason drove away still silent on the way back to Lafayette and Summers place. As they drove along Chartres Street she asked Jason to pull up as she wanted to walk the rest of the way on her own.

So without saying a word he pulled up by the turning off Canal Street. And watched her walk away up Canal Street till she was out of sight then continued his journey back to his place, for some reason he felt uneasy towards the end in the clinic, and then in the car. He couldn't put his finger on it. But it was when she kept hold his hand tight and more or less pulled him in to the room with the doctor. After all she'd said back at her place before coming about him not coming in as she wasn't ready for him to know all her secrets. He didn't even know what to say to her when it didn't work. And she swore something he'd never heard her say. He'd wait for her to contact him. Maybe after she's been to her session at the church with the father tonight she will be her self I hope so.

It was 10 45 am, and Maggie had not woke her up as usual early. As she opened her eye's to the sun blazing in through the window. Her head was splitting and she felt sick in the stomach with a foul tasty in her mouth, as she realised she was on the coach fully clothed. Sitting on the cupboard opposite was Maggie staring at her.

Whats up old girl why are you over there? Dragged herself to a sitting position, god her head ached. Looked at her watch it was nearly 11 but the sun was out? If my watch is correct it should still be 11pm at night and Wednesday. Leaned over and picked up her cell phone, and to her horror it was Thursday morning. She'd lost several hours of time. The last thing she remembered was driving with Jason to the clinic. She had a message on her phone, it was from the priest it seemed she missed her appointment at 8 last evening. What the hell I think I'm going mad as she stood up and walked towards Maggie who quickly ran into the spare room and under the bed.

Maggie I'd not hurt you, you know that so know need to be scared. I need some Panadol for my head walking into the kitchen and put the coffee on then walked into the bathroom to the medicine cupboard with its glass fronted door and stood num as she saw her mouth covered in what look like dried blood. Turned and walked into the bedroom and stood in front of the full lenght mirror, what she feared had happened, as she looked at herself her top torn and covered in again what looked like blood. Her left eye was red and she had a bruise on her arm. She tore at her top screaming till it came off in pieces, then her bra and trousers and walked back in the bathroom and jumped under the shower turning it to hot, got the soap and brush and scrubbed her body as hard as she could till it was red raw, as she felt unclean.

Suddenly she had a pain in her stomach and was violently sick in the shower. Tears were running down her face as she was so scared at what she might have done to get like this in 24 hours, as the shower washed away the sick.

She switched the shower off and put her towering robe on and walked back into the kitchen and got a black bag to put the torn clothes in. Picked up the pile of clothes and put them in the bag. Then walked over to the cat litter tray in the corner of the bathroom and tipped it into the bag poo and all. Left it tied up by the back door and poured herself a strong coffee and opened a tin of tune chunks and put it on the floor for her cat.

She went outside and sat on the veranda trying hard to remember yesterday. Only she couldn't, opened the packet of Panadol and took out two and stared at the rest of the pills wondering if she took them all would they take away the mental pain she felt just then, as well as her head and stomach pains? Took both pills, then another one, only she couldn't bring herself to take more. Took a sip off coffee and looked at the world around her. The Street was empty, it looked as if it had showered earlier, the air smelt fresh and clean unlike herself but still hot as she still felt dirty for some reason. Maggie came out and jumped up on her and rubber herself against her chest, she held her close and realised that the cat had smelt blood on her so she was scared. Also she didn't know if her other self even liked Maggie.

The heat of the morning started to settle in for the day at 40 c, the rain had helped a little with the humidity as it started to rain again, not heavy but was enough to soak you if you were out in it. Only the way she felt the rain was comforting for some reason. Sorry Maggie but I'm going to get dressed and I have to go out to see the priest, I'll bring you back some fresh cooked chicken.

Summer stood in Jackson Square and looked up at St Louis Cathedral looming over the square all white and magnificent and hesitated as she had know Ideal how she was going to explain yesterday to the father. Only he was her only chance of being normal. Other wise she'd jump in the Mississippi River and drown herself, which would be easy as she couldn't swim, hoping her other self couldn't swim or stop her.

She put one foot in front of the other and walked up the steps in to the body of the church. To the left was the Virgin Mary and child just inside the door and she knelt in front of it and prayed hard then crossed herself and took her crucifix from around her neck and held it tight to her chest as she walked up to the Alter and stood in front of Jesus statue and crossed herself. A voice behind her made her turn around. It was the Father pleased to see she was there, but wanted to know why she hadn't come last evening.

Summer blurted out fast every thing to him. Tears had started running down her checks. He led her into the Rectory at the back to a chair and got her a glass of water from the large Industrial water bottle that sat on a stand in a corner.

He took his own well loved tatty bible that was used by him for years and put his crucifix around it. Then took her hand in his and held it on top of the bible in his other hand and said some holy words in latin. Then he asked her to repeat what she just said but slowly and more clearly.

After repeating what she remembered and about her clothes and bruises.

Is that why you have sun glass's on miss?

Ye's Father my black eye. I had bruises a couple of years back after a memory loose that lasted only a few hours. This one was 23 hours. It has never lasted that long before.

The trigger is stress course by an incident. The visit to the doctor to be Hypnotised was the reason yes? I'm sure your doctor would agree. So maybe if you told her, then she could help you and find out what happened to you to get your black eye. You would have to try not to get stressed before going. Would you like to read a passage out of the bible, letting go of her hand and got up and got her a new bible. See you don't have the one I gave you that first day with you.

It wasn't where I keep it this morning. I was in a hurry to come here to look for it Father sorry?

Thats fine handing her the new one. And for half an hour she read a passage out of it. The priest blessed her and read a passage that dealt with getting rid of demons. Over and over for 30 minutes then a gain blessed her. And then the session was over and the father was drained, his wrinkled face white as a sheet. He'd never read that passage before to her but he knew he had to try as it was the last straw, as he looked at her unhappy face. He knew the Church would not have approve but he felt he had to try.

I want you to come again tomorrow around about this time and we'll do all this again and each morning in the hope it works miss.

As she got up to leave a news headline caught her eye on his deck, It read that last night a man's body was found with his throat ripped, this is the forth murder like this in the last 3 years. The police believe it is a wild animal that can't find his usual prey and is attacking venerable people. It asked for people to be weary while out late. And keep pets inside at night. Summer face went white as a sheet, turned and looked at the Father. You don't think that was me last night?

Not a tall if you read it right it said a wild animal not a human. Do you really think you're capitol of doing something like that, because I don't so put your mind at rest.

As she left the Church, she couldn't get the newspaper article out of her head as she headed along Decatur Street towards the Central Grocery to buy a Muffuletta, as it was well past lunchtime. Her headache had gone and her stomach felt better so she hoped to keep it down.

The shop was full of southern spices and noodles of every kind on the shelves and tins of stuff she'd never heard of. The shop was just what you pictured in your mind when you thought about New Orleans and Grocery's. There was a small Mall near the Casino but it didn't sell food only expensive clothes. Waiting in line for it to be made she was glad New Orleans still had old fashioned places like this, as she dislike Supermarkets?

Holding her hot Muffuletta in her hand she walked back to the square and in to the grounds in the centre of it to sit under a tree in the shade to eat it while listening to music from a band outside the Church there in the square.

As she finished it, she thought about what the Father had said, and had come to a decision to be Hypnotise, as she had to know what had happen to course her clothes to be covered in blood and ripped, also the black eye and bruises. She felt good about continue with the Father, as he had a way of putting her mind at rest, only not this time because of the blood. As she knew It wasn't hers, so who the hell was it she had to know?

Taking out her cell phone she phoned the Doctor and said she'd keep her next appointment as her other self took over outside the clinic before she'd even gone inside. So I believe that is why it didn't work. The doctor was pleased she was going to try again and would look forward to their next session. Summer felt a little better knowing she was at least trying to get herself well.Then phoned Jason as she'd not heard from him and that was unusual.

Jason hadn't be able to settle since dropping her off after the Clinic. He couldn't bring himself to see her, as he was nerves that she hadn't been herself again. Like that first evening way back when she'd turned up unexpected very late and seduced him. Although she was a virgin and had made it very clear before hand that she didn't believe in free sex unless they were an item which at the time they weren't.

Then to wake the next morning to find she'd just left without a word. Then later when they met it was as if it hadn't happened, and she never mentioned it again. Then when they did finally make love as an item, she didn't even remember that they had already had sex before. At the time I dismissed it but after yesterday I just can't.

Just then his phone went and saw it was Summer, he ignore her and picked up a couple of glass's and walked over to the bar. The bar was nearly empty because of the rain and humidity out side so he didn't have a lot to do and some of his staff were on vacation else where. Only now after her phoning he couldn't get her out of his mind and decided to text her instead of speaking on it.

Summer was disappointed that Jason hadn't answered her call. She'd decided to go see him at the Balcony Club bar. She had to explain as much as she could leaving out the blood and bruises. She hoped he'd listen and not think her mad.

A taxi was coming towards her with his sign up so knew he was empty so stuck out her hand for him to stop. Walking wasn't an option for her the way she felt, and she was scared that she'd could loose her memory at any time now and not be able to stop it.

Outside Jason's place, she paid the taxi and walked up to the doors. She so hoped he'd let her explain herself, now she knew she wasn't herself yesterday when she was with him. And she didn't want to loose his friendship if she could help it.

Jason was deep in conversation with a bleach blonde well built young woman, who was just about wearing a strapless mini dress, and didn't notice her walk in to the bar.

There wern't many in there she noticed looking around, about a dozen young guys listen to a Jazz band while drinking long cool glass's of larger, and the one bussom bleach blonde woman.

Her blood was boiling as she watched them laughing together as Jason put his hand on the woman's arm as they sipped red wine together.

For the first time she was jealous and wanted to claw the woman's eyes out. A feeling she'd never felt before. She realised the only time she was ever angry was that last evening with her stepfather and didn't like the feeling. Turned and walked back out the way she had come in and stood on the veranda, her mind was full of questions. As she suddenly realised she was feeling the way her other self felt, angry and if she was right, that her memory only went when things got too hot for her to handle or that her other self didn't like. Like the clinic but not the Church which was strange? Why didn't she lose her memory when she saw Jason canoodling freely with a blonde at the bar? In stead she felt all the bad emotion for the first time.

So what was different about yesterday and today? Father reading the passage for getting rid of demons, which he read over and over again. That was the only thing she could think of. It had to that what else could it be?

For the first time in over three years she felt there was a brake though with her identity disorder. Took out her sell phone from her pocket and phoned the Father to tell him what she believed had just happened, sat down on the steps of the bar as she phoned and waited excited at the prospect of being cured.

Father listened to every word, then asked her to call at the church at 6 tonight and go though that passage again. And if she was okay with it to come again in the morning around 11 as you have a gig tonight don't you Summer? I'm afraid I have to go now I'll see you at 6 God bless you my child.

Summer found herself holding her crucifix in her other hand the silver chain hanging loosely around her neck as she said goodbye to the Father she'd not realised she'd been holding all the while she was on the phone. Got up and walked down the rest of the steps and away from the bar towards Esplanade Avenue then across it and up to North Rampart Street and through Louis Armstrong Park to home. And for the first time she felt different inside, as if she were now in control of her mind and body. She had a gig to prepare for and was looking forward to singing at the Casino, she'd eat in there restaurant before going on. It was free and she'd not taken them up on it before.

Friday morning came around and she woke with a start, looked at her watch she'd just about have time to feed Maggie who was still curled up on top of Summers legs, unlike yesterday, and shower cleared up after herself and grab breakfast on the run before her session at the Church.

Last night went so well that she'd stayed behind to talk music business with Marshall and some people in the music business world. And wasn't driven home till gone 3 am, so no wonder it was now 10 17am.

After a rush she was ready as the taxi she'd ordered before she'd showered drew up outside. Kissed Maggie and left.

Father Mathew was pleased she'd had a good evening, even more pleased she had handled her emotion at Jasons place. He went throw the same passages as yesterday and then blessed her with holy water. They then sat in the Church with a coffee and chatted, He wanted to no more about how she felt during the years with her stepfather? Was she never angry with him?

Summer explained that from the start he had made it clear that if she ever told anyone, a part from the fact that he was Mayor, no one would believe a child, he'd have her sent to a mental institute till she stoped telling lies. She was far too young to know he couldn't do that.

So of course was scared of him and spent most of her childhood isolated from other school children after school. Even her bedroom was no sanitary so she realised that she had know choice but have to put up with him. She was only 15 when she left home, if you can call it that. Coming here I felt at ease for the first time. No longer scared but free at last and happy.

The Father thought about what she had just told him. And came to the conclusion that when something bad invaded her peaceful life, that was when her mind split in two and gave her another identity.

And now your mind is healing it self with the help of God and prayer, and you feeling anger for the first time in your life shows it its working. There is one thing child you must never tell anyone about the ritual from the Bible that I am using, as it is forbidden by the church unless you get permission from the Vatican.

Summer smiled and told him that what happened in Church stayed in Church, only God will know. I will see you on our next session and thankyou Father you have given me my life back. How can I ever repay you?

When you're a famous singer remember New Orleans homeless and help maintain our hostel we started during the Covid-19 outbreak in the old empty Hotel with a donation. And thankyou for the money you left last night in the poor box.

Of course I'll do all I can to help she replied. Do you know that Los Angeles has over 40 thousand homeless, I was taken by car around where they all seem to collect after dark. So much for Movie glamour City?

I'm afraid homeless is the curse of every City in every Country, we do what we can in our own back yard here. Now I'm afraid I have another appointment Summer.

Outside the Church she felt even more positive as she walked through the square and across St Ann's to the Restaurant on the corner of the square, as she knew they made pancake and omelet's which were very thick and big with lots of different toppings. She'd have a cheese and onion omelet before visiting the Pit-bull rescue centre, as she wanted to see if they had any other breeds of dogs besides Pit-bulls as she realised her relationship with Jason was now over as he'd not phoned her. And she'd always wanted a dog.
She was sure Maggie wouldn't mind as she had enough love for both, and she'd treat her just the same as always. She'd take the dog with her too gigs and for walks. And if it was a big dog it would

stop men trying to get off with her, and she'd not feel angry or every loose her memory which she hoped wouldn't ever happen again.

She had been fine in herself for a week and it was the day of the Doctors appointment, So far she'd got to the reception area of the Clinic without any incident, and her mind was normal fingers crossed. Doctor Novikou came out of her office and greeted her and lead her into her office and to a chair this time.

No boyfriend this time summer? 'Pleased that he wasn't there"

We aren't together any more.

CHAPTER 9

Are you sure you really want to do this before we start?

Ye's I have to but first no recording.

Even after what happened last time?

Ye's I have to know what I do when not my self.

Okay so now we can get started, there is one thing miss you will remember it all while you're Hypnotised. I'll not use the rotating light this time. Close your eyes and clear your mind, then open them and stare straight head of you concentration on an object straight in front of you.We'll start with the time you lost last Wednesday. So let's get started, now keep staring ahead.

Summer looked straight ahead, and after a couple of minutes was under Hypnotise.

Now Summer take your mind back to Wednesday morning outside the Clinic with your boyfriend, about to come in.

Summer saw herself reluctant to go inside and let herself be Hypnotised. She pretended to go under for a short while, then made it clear she wasn't and decided to leave and go back to the French Quarter and enjoy herself doing something different. She'd had enough of Jason, there was no way she wanted to be tired down, at least not for a long time, after holding his hand really tightly although the session and then ignoring him at the same time. Maybe he'd get the message so that when I retreat back inside of myself he will let her know he wasn't happy the way things are between them right now? He was a terrible lay anyway.

Once back out side she started to walk through the Quarter a place she really loved. Got herself a coach tour ticket for the afternoon to see 2 Plantation Mansions maybe one of the owner will be around at one of them. And give me a private viewing who knows. I need something else for fun beside's singing.

Summer saw herself eating lunch, then after lunch the coach tour of over 3 hours of touring different Plantation's. Without any luck with the owner's she was bored stiff. Looked at her watch it was still early at only 4 30, to go to the Casino and play the fruit machines, maybe I might even get lucky with a pick up of a wealthy business guy and have some fun in the bedroom at the Casino's Hotel. For now I'll walk to the Mall and pass the time there. I know the Casino is open all ready but the rich men won't be there yet she told herself.

After walking around the Mall opposite the Casino, she decided to buy herself something nice at a designer clothes shop, an expensive long silk scarf before going to the Casino. She hoped the expensive looking shopping bag with the stores name on would give the impression that she was rich and maybe attract a rich man.

Here goes nothing as she walked into the place. Even at gone 6 37 pm it had people playing the fruit machine. There was none free for her to play yet so decided to grab a bite at the coffee shop inside the place and bide her time till one was free. She had plenty of time as the card and roulette wheel didn't get started till 8 pm. And the big players didn't start to play till around 9 to 9 30.

Luckily Marshall wasn't there yet. She hoped he'd not be in tonight, as he'd most likely notice her and start up a conversation. She didn't want him to come near while she was different in her mind. She liked what she'd seen of him when her other self sang there. He was a perfectly honest gentleman, unlike the prevues CEO here. He wasn't honest or nice, and a complete coward when confronted by me she remembered. Died squealing like a pig. Unlike the others they all put up a fight, although they had started it in the first place. All but Jason's Mother, that one was fun doing.

Luckily she has me to defend her. Good now I see a fruit machine empty. After just over an hour she'd won enough as the fruits lined up, she had a stake in chips to go on the Black Jack table as the place was filling up with the big money punters. She'd watch for a while before joining, see who has money to burn by his playing.

After another hour she'd taken up a seat at the table. Blackjack was her game and she was good at it. Not that her other self ever played it much herself. Playing for a while she'd not had any luck with finding a rich business man. And was about to give up and cash in when a tall guy with his dark brown hair in a ponytail wearing an handmade dark grey suit and a black string tie joined them. God he was beautiful and even taller than herself as he sat at the table.

He sat opposite her and lay a roll of notes on the table. The Croupier counted it and gave him a lot of chips before shuffling the new deck of card's. She wouldn't mind him under her sheets tonight looking at the guy. He also looked straight at her and smiled before putting the chips in several piles. She only had 2 piles but most of the 2 piles were her winnings.

After a couple of hour's the guy had won a fair few hands, and it seemed to her that his pile never seemed to go down so she decided to call it quits before she lost all her's. And just sat and watched for a while with a nice glass of Chablis wine courtesy of the guy, it also came with a note asking her to have supper with him at his place later. Making her think she was well in there, as this could be her rich guy.

Decided to go cash in her chips and come back and stand and watch from a short distance.

Midnight came and went, and the guy had a tracked a lot of people around the table as he was winning big time. So much so Marshall had been called. Summer on seeing him enter hide herself in the crowd around the guy, as she didn't want him to see her.

Two am came around and Marshall had the table closed as the place would close soon.

She decided to wait outside for him near the parked cars out side the Casino, wondering which one was his? She did not have long to wait as he came outside the casino and walked towards her, as she stood beside a large greek pillar and waited her silk scarf around her head and neck so know one would know her face. Only he could tell it was her because of the outfit he recognised, also that she was tall like him with her heels.

As he got near she stepped in front of him and smiled waiting for him to introduce himself and then lead her to his car. He said his name was Brandon and he was from New York and then waited for her to tell him her name.

I'm called Cristal and I'm from Seattle. Niceties over, they walked to his shiny black sports car. "A Mercedes" she froze in front of the open car door, as Mercedes was her real name as a shiver went done her spin. If only she'd taken notice of the feeling of doom she felt right then, but no instead she climbed in and buckled up as he switch the powerful engine on and drove off in the direction of Audubon Park where millionaire houses stood.

She sat silent as they pulled up outside a Mansion type large house in a street of the same, all with wrought iron fencing and verandas all painted white.

My bolt hole what do you think pretty girl? And leaned over her opening her door then he got out his side. She noticed a sickly sweet smell coming from him as he did so. She suddenly wished she'd gone home after playing cards at the Casino but it was too late now as he stood by his gate swinging his keys in his hand waiting for her.

She got out and walked past him and up the path to the front door. She could feel his breath on her neck as he'd got close, as he leaned his body against her and put the key in the door. She could feel his heart beating as they started to walk inside.

Inside the place was very eighth century in decor as was the furniture. She liked the look so far as she was bodily hustled into a large sitting room with a large beautiful marble fireplace. The 60 inch television over it spoilt it she felt.

Brandon poured her a large glass of light brownish liquid from a decanter, then himself a small one and led her by the arm to a regency style coach which looked very uncomfortable so she declined and started walking around looking at the paintings and ornaments trying to keep at arm's length from him.

Surely Cristal you'r not scared of me, you seemed up for it in the Casino other wise why wait for me near my car?

There was something about him away from the Casino, she couldn't put her finger on but felt he was dangerous, she was glad that she had a 5th degree black belt in Kickboxing. So if there is any funny business she would be able to take care of myself so girl pull yourself together as she poured the drink in to a fancy jug on a side table when he wasn't looking. And enjoy the rest of the night she told herself before answering him. I don't normally drink spirit leaving the glass on a small table. I Was just enjoying your home, as I'v never had the pleasure to be inside a place like this before. I live in a brick built house, you know solid walls.

Brandon smiled then to her surprise said let us get down to business shall we walking into the hall and stood at the bottom of an ornate large set of sweeping white stairs. You're here for one thing sex so shall we, as he took a step to one side at the bottom of the stairs and put his hand out for her to go up them.

Right now sex was the last thing on her mind, she'd gone pass it after that initial bad feeling by his car. And the way he talked without any softness or desire in it. Just matter of fact. Sex should be fun you should both want to ripe each others clothes off and start to caress each others body's.

She got the feeling that wasn't how he felt about it.

If you don't mind it's late I have an early start in the morning at the music studio"not true but he didn't know that" I'll call a taxi and wait by your gate if you don't mind she said turning to wards the front door? Maybe some other time yes?

His face change to anger as he took a step towards her. I do mind as I need you right now, even if your not going to let me fuck you in my bedroom on my bed? Bend over and hold onto that cupboard while I pull your slacks and pants down and fuck you from the back as he grabbed her arm. You can't let a bloke believe he's going to play sex games with you, then change your mind for no good reason. Who the fuck do you think you are. I can get any girl I want, and right now it's you do you understand Cristal. We are going to have a long night of sex games starting right here. Right now your take all your clothes off and bend over, then after I'v fucked you up your back passage your go up where my bedroom awaits with all its sex gadgets. I'll have you screaming with pleasure from all the things I am going to do you by the time the night is over you'r see.

She looked him straight in the eye and asked why waste time down here as your room sound fascinating, so why not have your way with my body in comfort?

Brandon let go of her arm and put his hand out in front of her to show her the way as she started walking up the stairs with him at her heels.

His bedroom come playroom was at the back of the house, the door was at least 3 inches thick wood as he opened it holding it open for her to enter.

She'd never been in or seen a room like this, It had a round bed right in the centre of the room with no headboard but handcuffs attached to chains hanging around the outside of the bed. The walls had whip's hanging up and artificial thick cocks. Rubber mouth gags and black leather face masks. The room's walls were painted red with black drapes every where. She noticed that the window was boarded up and a black lace curtain hung down it. Do you bring many girls up here as she moved a good distance away from him.

When I come down for a weekend or so, after all the girls come here from all over the States to have a good time, most are brainless and so it makes it easy. I'm beginning to think you're not one of them? So tonight might be a little different with you.

I see you like red, I'v have never been in a room where the walls are painted red she replied.

Makes it easer if there is any blood splatter. She'd been here before with guys wanted sex anyway they could get it. Only Brandon was a little different. Still she believed she could handle him just like the others.

Brandon took a black whip off the wall and held it out in front of her. Get on and strip my cock will start to soften then your have to suck it a bit before I can fuck you. Then the fun can start.

My name is Mercedes and I don't suck or fuck pigs like you as she swung her leg up to his hand holding the whip, and knocked it out of it. Then instantly she swung around and kicked him in the stomach knocking him off his feet. Stood over him as he tried to get up and kneeled down on his stomach and handcuffed him with the one hanging above him on the side of the bed.

He swore at her several times, telling her that when he got free he'd cut her up in little piece and feed her to the gators like the others, trying hard to stand.

She kicked him in the head knocking him out cold for a while, giving her time to look around the room, and walked over to two large cupboards. The first one held trinkets, watch's and woman's things all in neat piles and labeled in woman's first names. A terrible thought crossed her mind, that he was a serial killer of young girls. Without a second thought she walked out onto the landing then down stairs and looked around for the kitchen as there were so many doors. Found it and looked for a sharp meat knife. Found a large sharp one and a small equal shape pairing knife, and went back up stairs as she knew just what to do to him. As she wasn't going to kill him not this time.

Brandon was still out cold so she moved his leg nearer the bed and handcuffed his foot to it. So much for all those chains with handcuffs attached as you are going to get a taste of your own medicine pretty boy she smiled.

Layed the knives on to top of the bed by his head and begun to take his trousers down then his pants. His willy was tiny by now laying in a tuft of red pubic hair. Got hold of his willy and took the pairing knife and begun to cut it, but his testicles kept getting in the way so got the bigger knife and begun to cut them off first.

He suddenly woke screaming out in pain.

You don't like someone inflicting pain on you but you don't mind doing it to others, as she took the gag off the hook on the wall as he continued to scream and shoved it into his mouth and tied it up at the back of his head. Now peace at last as I get on with cutting your sexual organs off.

After 20 minutes they were off and on the floor beside him. She Looked at herself in the full length mirror on the red wall and saw she was covered in blood. Stripped off her outfit and stood over him her virginia in his face. Is this what you wanted bending over him and rubbed it over his face, got up and walked into the adjoining shower room and showered the blood off herself, dried herself with his towels and put on the his red dressing gown and black slippers which surprising to her they fitted, he must have small feet like his cock, as she took size 7?

She calmly rapped the bloody clothes in the bath towel and went down stairs and put them in the washing machine, then put them on hot cycle and put powder in it. And watch for a second as it started to rotate. Got a bucket and mope from the laundry room and filled it with hot water and soap powdered already used in the machine. And cleaned every where she'd been or touched.

She'd noticed a laundry bag in the room so put the glass she'd held now clean in to it, and waited for the laundry to finish then dry so she could put the outfit back on. She past the time wearing rubber gloves she'd found in a draw full of dozens all large. She went though the whole house from top to bottom. And went though his deck in his office. He had a safe in the wall behind a painting of an elderly man, and started to twiddle with the it till she heard clicks, after a while it opened.

Inside were a stack of girls identity cards and credit cards, several Visa cards in different names. And a large bundle of money. Some of it was what he had won that evening at the Casino. She took the money and put it in the laundry bag. Then looked through the documents inside. It seemed he'd inherited the house from his father who inherited it from his. They came from old money. It seemed he'd not had to work a day in his life. She was angry and just wanted to get out of the place, her clothes should be dry by now and went to check.

Went back upstairs to check on him and took the gag off. He was unconscious. Decided to look in the other cupboard in the room, She wasn't ready for what she found inside several hat boxing, as she opened one looking up at her was the terrified face of what was once a beautiful girl, Opened the end one and there was the same inside and knew the rest must contain the same because on top of the cupboard were several empty ones. She couldn't wait to get out of there looking at him, at least the men I kill deserved it unlike you, you bastard kicking him in the head and left.

Half an hour later after checking that she'd not forgot to clean everything that she may have touched she walked out in his back garden and over several back gardens to a street a couple of streets away from his house carrying the laundry bag with the bath towel and other stuff to put in one of the industrial bins behind the office block on her way home.

Made a short detour to the homeless shelter, on the way there past some homeless men laying in shop door ways and peeled a couple of 100 dollar notes off the pile of dollars notes she'd found in his Safe and gave them the money. At the homeless hotel the doors were always open, so nipped inside and put the same amount beside the head of each sleeping homeless man. There were no woman funny that she thought. She'd give the rest to the Father for him to use it for the needy as there was a lot since the pandemic. She wanted no part in the dirty money. Now a slow walk home as her legs were aching from all the walking. She knew this might be her last time being her other self as she felt different calmer for the first time.

When she had come out of being Hypnotised, She'd relived the whole thing as if she were there. The doctor had been silent as she'd just heard that she'd had hurt someone called Brandon. And evidently done it several times before. She knew there was nothing she could do about it as she was bound by her oath, she'd loose her license to work if she did. And her patient had said that they all deserved to die and she knew a few who would fit the bill herself. How do you feel miss, has that helped you?

Summer got up and asked for her taps of the session. And reminded her of her oath. She took the whole audio machine and tape's of that whole mornings sessions. Then thanked the doctor and walked out to reception and paid the bill in cash then left. Leaving the doctor wondering if what she'd heard was real.

Summer walked down Canal Street then along Riverwalk till she came to the steps leading up into Jackson Square. Got a coffee from the cafe by the steps and went and sat in the garden of the square next to the Church. Music was playing from a band on the square and the Artist's we're out in full. Large colourful Parasols were up every where to keep the heat of the day off the Artist and the band. Summer sat out of the heat on a bench under a tree and thought about what she had just relived.

She'd put her real name of Mercedes out of her mind when she moved there, and had be came Summer complete in every way, shutting out fear or anger just living for her music. But the world isn't like that as it can be a cruel violent place, and can try and get at you, Only she had refused to face that side of her life. So that was were her other identity came in, and took charge of that side of her life for nearly four years.

And a lot had happened since then, some nice some not so. What would it serve to come clean about the murders her other self had committed it wouldn't bring them back, and she knew now that they were all bad people anyway, committing crimes them selves?

And who would believe she had a split personality disorder, they would put her away in a mad house for the rest of her life. Who would that serve not herself, she'd die if she couldn't play and sing her music she'd rather be dead.

Now she was ready to face the world as her whole self once more. No more loss of memory, and if anyone try's anything bad with me I am ready to handle it as my true self. And when the dog I am getting from the Rescue kennel Pit-bull and paroles. And the dog has had its checkup he'll be with me 24/7 so men should leave me well alone with an Alsatian by my side. So I don't have to resort to hurting any body hopefully anymore?

This is going to be the start of my new life at 21, and with my music CD's starting to sell all over the State's now, and with better gigs in bigger better City's on the cards. I'll not let anyone get in my way on my way to the top with my music. Now I could do with a meal, something with red meat that I can get my teeth into getting up to find a Restaurant.

Brandon was still in his Mansion only now dead, as he'd bleed to death. As he had no friends there, so no one missed him. The newspaper headlines about the animal attack on a man, killing him. Father Mathew had read in Thursday's newspaper said it turned out to be just that an animal. The reported said that the police had said the teeth marks showed just that. He also reported that the police were know were near solving the other so called animal attacks over the past 3 years or so. Father put the newspaper to one side to show Summer tonight when she came for her reading. Hoping it would put her mind at rest, that there was no way she'd kill the man .Crossing himself thanking God for helping her.

Printed in Great Britain
by Amazon